SHORELINE OF INFINITY

Awa
fictic
in S
Univ

SCOTLAND'S FESTIVAL OF SCIENCE FICTION, FANTASY & HORROR WRITING

ISSUE 39:
SUMMER 2025

ISSN: 2059-2590
ISBN: 978-1-7395359-5-7

Submissions of fiction, art, reviews, poetry, non-fiction are welcomed: visit the website to find out how to submit

www.shorelineofinfinity.com

Publisher
Shoreline of Infinity Publications /
The New Curiosity Shop
Edinburgh
Scotland

210525

EDITORIAL TEAM

Co-founders:
Noel Chidwick,
Mark Toner

Editor-in-Chief:
Noel Chidwick

Editorial Team:

Fiction Editor:
Eris Young

Reviews Editor:
Ann Landmann

Non-fiction Editor:
Pippa Goldschmidt

Production Editor:
Noel Chidwick,

Copy-editors:
Pippa Goldschmidt
Iain Maloney
Eris Young
Cat Hellisen

and thanks to our
excellent readers

CONTENTS

COVER ART

Vincent Kings

FIRST CONTACT

www.shorelineofinfinity.com
contact@shorelineofinfinity.com
Also on Instagram & Bluesky

Ten Years After...

...releasing Shoreline of Infinity One in June 2015

...the launch event of Shoreline of Infinity One, which became the first Event Horizon,

what has changed in ten years? In the words of Remember Monday, "What the Hell just Happened?"

In Scotland, UK and worldwide, so much: Brexit, Johnson & Truss, two dump loads of Trump, Covid, Ukraine, Gaza, other wars popping up all over the planet, the worsening effects of the climate catastrophe ... and 'AI.' Ruth EJ Booth's piece (p106) "Hold The Chicken: The Argument Against AI Art" eloquently takes you through the many reasons why Generative AI 'Art' is nothing of the sort.

Ten years ago robots creating art was science fiction - ten years after? it still is, but the big tech bros are building the machinery to force it down our throats, after sucking all the creative juices out of our writers and artists. What to do?

Keep it analogue, keep it real. We began our regular live events by accident, when Russell Jones said we must have a launch for Issue One. The launch was a band playing SF songs, SF poetry, readings. For me, the eye opener was Debbie Cannon reading one of the stories from issue one. Debbie is a very talented Scottish actor who I have been privelaged to get to know and work with on assorted projects ever since.

We've run around 100 Event Horizons in the ten years, with an audiences of real people enjoying the performances of real people. As any actor or musician will tell you, the thrill of performing to a live audience cannot be beaten. Latterly, I've enjoyed running simple events of writers reading to audiences, up close and personal. Getting back to telling stories around the campfire. This is true art, human to human, sharing and distilling experiences and imagination.

Generative AI is a dead-end. It is already heading to becoming Douglas Adam's nightmare disco of androids dancing with androids.

Let's keep it human, people.

Dreamers – not 'droids.

—Noel Chidwick
Co-founder, Editor-in-Chief
Shoreline of Infinity
SF Caledonia

PULL UP A LOG

Remembrance Eve

Anna Ziegelhof

This is now: I begin the day at the tea vendor's shop. Not much has changed. The airy space – half inside, half outside, bright and minimal – still exudes calm. There are more unknown faces now than when I was a regular. It's been five years. Not that long, in the grand scheme of things, but an entire life has been added to my consciousness since I left.

Patrons are conversing quietly on floor cushions. I look around and my gaze stumbles over a familiar figure. This particular memory comes from my own life, not the one that was added to my consciousness: it's Briar, who arrived here from a world so different I couldn't grasp it. She challenged me, attracted me, pushed me away; she finally tricked me and set me on the irreversible path I chose, of becoming a Witness.

"Welcome back, Ce!" The tea vendor comes around the counter to greet me; a welcome excuse to turn away and pretend I didn't see Briar. "We are so glad to have you with us today."

"Thank you, Yan. It's an honor."

Yan assesses me through half-closed eyes. Seeing xer observe me, present and attuned, feels like home, a memory distinctly from my own life, not the implant.

There is something Yan can see about a person, in addition to their body: their self, their needs, perhaps, their state of mind. Seeing me today, xe winces – the look of someone sympathetic to pain they've just witnessed.

"You really carry two lives now, don't you? I'll make you something."

Yan returns to xer workstation behind the counter.

Xe's right, of course. I carry two lives now. One is the serene life with memories of growing up here, on a recovering planet, in a welcoming little town, near friendly forests and sustaining meadows. The other is a life from our past, overcome not too long ago. Both remembered lives feel equally real to me, as far as memories can be considered real.

Yan prepares my tea. I've always enjoyed watching xer at work, but today, with an implanted past in me, xer small gestures carry even more significance: in this life, my life, I was always able to allow the tea vendor to read my state of mind. I never had to hide aspects of myself for fear of being turned into the authorities for quick cash; in this life, I am safe to enter a state of meditative focus while watching Yan gather herbs and spices from xer many drawers. I don't have to be hyper-alert, worrying about how I look, how I stand, how I speak, lest someone pin meaning on an unconscious mannerism and file an accusation against me.

The crisp clang of miniscule brass weights reminds me that I am safe in this tea shop. I won't spiral into panic because I have to wait in a public space in full view of strangers.

The fine-tuned scales move into equilibrium. This metaphor, in this world, in this moment, reminds me of all the work I did during Witness-training to bring my two lives into a balance.

Heat wafts off the roasting pan. It's benevolent and contained, not the heat of arson.

Cardamom pods crack and their warm aroma fills the air. I allow the scent to calm me; I am not gasping in shallow breaths knowing I am inhaling burnt flesh.

A few twists of the pestle – not the tightening of screws around skulls – then the spice blend rustles into the pot.

Water sizzles, steam interlaces with sunlight. Yan resets xer workstation while sand trickles through the timer.

Idle time, no rush, no hustle. This is now: I am in my hometown and present in my life, in both my lives.

"Lest we forget, rest where we are, steer where we go," Yan recites. Xe hands me the teacup. I thank xer and return the holiday greeting.

"Falling or catching?" I ask xer.

"Falling, for all my fallen siblings," xe responds.

"I'll catch you."

This is now and it's time to stop pretending I didn't see Briar. She looks up from her book when I approach her table and blushes.

"How have you been?" seem like good enough first words.

"Good." Her voice is still raspy. Permanent damage, I know now. She never told me what happened, but I've known since Remembrance Eve, five years ago.

We speak at the same time:

"So you're back – so you're still –"

We chuckle at the same time.

I remember how the delicate skin around her eyes wrinkles when she laughs. I remember her long lashes and that one emerald speck inside her iris.

"Join me for a moment?" she offers.

"Thank you."

"So you're back," she says.

"So you're still here," I say.

✧

Remembrance Eve, five years ago: I began the day at the tea vendor's shop and ran into Briar, then, too. We hadn't spoken since breaking up, but it was Remembrance Eve, the atmosphere delicate and conciliatory. I was raw with grief for Mary and out of my mind with worry about a future without people like Mary to remind us of the past; a future in which we might forget. My quarrels with Briar seemed puny, so I didn't turn away when she approached me.

"I was so sorry to hear about Mary's passing," she said.

"Thank you. It's been hard."

We drank sheepish sips of tea.

"What will you be doing now?"

"I've been wrapping up Mary's affairs, documenting and preserving her art, writing a lot. I don't know yet what's next."

I had been Mary's assistant. I helped her with the project of recording her memories. As she advanced in age, I became her nurse. Her passing, a few weeks prior to that Remembrance Eve, five years ago, had not been unexpected, but my grief was still acute.

"I'm worried," I confessed to Briar that morning. "We are transitioning to a time in which nobody alive still remembers the Score period. It's a precarious moment."

"Today is special," Briar stated. I met her eyes. Alert and interested, yet also emotionless and unreadable. I felt that familiar jab of annoyance that she never allowed a softening, not even on a vulnerable day like this.

"You're right. Remembrance is special."

"I didn't know Mary long, but I know she was extraordinary," Briar said. "And I know how much she meant to you."

"She was our last primary, the last person to still personally remember…" I went silent. My constantly explaining things to Briar was part of the reason we broke up.

Briar had arrived as a refugee from off-planet. I was on her welcoming team. I showed her around, helped her learn to accommodate her injuries, practiced language with her, explained things about life in our town, our culture. But I never snapped out of it when we got involved romantically. She'd lose patience with me: "Can we just go eat without it becoming a lecture about economy and sustainability? I know I'm from a shit place. I notice the differences. You don't have to constantly rub them in. I want to learn, but sometimes I just want to go out to dinner with my girlfriend."

"We are losing our primaries," I said, skipping an explanation. "It frightens me. Some are still alive in other towns. The Witnesses are working hard on recording their memories, but I don't know if the Witness program is enough. Not many join it. How long until we get rid of it entirely? How long until Remembrance Eve becomes a hollow rite nobody takes seriously anymore?"

It was our first Remembrance Eve without a primary, wouldn't it be like watching something vaguely relevant but detached from our experience?

With Mary still around, the connection to our past was always in the amphitheater with us. If we felt the need to talk, we were able to talk to Mary, who remembered the Deviance Score system. She survived it, but as she got older, I realized that Score was the wound that governed her life. As she aged, she spoke about it more and more often, sometimes as if it weren't over.

"Are you falling or catching?" Briar asked me.

"Falling," I answered. "Feels important to fall this year."

Falling is awful, but I felt like I needed to make a statement after losing Mary. I was afraid that soon voices would ask, "Why are we putting ourselves through that?" I was afraid that eventually voices would ask, "When will we be allowed to move on from the past?"

"Me too," Briar said.

"What?"

"I'm falling too. I'm joining the first-timers."

"You don't have to!" tumbled out of me. "Nobody expects you to! It's entirely voluntary! You're still…"

"I'm still what?"

Still limping, wheezing, wincing, unable to hold a teacup with her injured hand…

Another issue between Briar and me: it had once been my task to take care of her. Whenever I looked at her, I also still saw a memory of her on the day she first arrived. I met her in the common room of the community house, where she had been given a room. She seemed so small, for someone who had been, I was told, a soldier in a conflict off-planet that seemed utterly far away and unrelated to our world. She was a small, grey, injured person who seemed perfectly exhausted but forcibly alert, like someone on the run.

I never stopped wanting to protect her.

"I'm going to do it," she said. "I'm sick of being the leech, the village-invalid."

She was still calling herself hateful names. She still thought she would need to pay us back. She still didn't believe that we welcomed people and shared resources freely.

She took a deep breath when she saw my glare.

"I'm valued," she recited, clearly quoting conclusions arrived at with her therapist. "My job is to heal and to arrive and to decide which profession feels aligned, to see if I want to stick around."

But she sounded sarcastic and my anger rose.

"Don't fall for the wrong reasons," I said. "It's hard. It's about remembering what motivates us. It's about putting yourself into a productive relationship with the past. Seriously, falling takes a lot out of you."

"It won't even be my own memory. How hard can it be?"

Her jaw muscle worked when she was angry.

I was angry, too. She still used her past as the stencil through which she saw reality. I had tried so hard to make her feel welcome and safe, trusted and appreciated, yet she steadfastly refused to open up to me, to us.

"Fine. Your decision. See you tonight," I said before anything angrier than that could come out. I left the tea shop. That was the last time I spoke to her until today, five years later.

This is now.

"I couldn't help but think of the last time I ran into you here," I say to Briar.

"Last time, yea. Long time ago."

We speak at the same time:

"I've been – how is."

We chuckle.

"Go ahead," I say.

"How is being a Witness?"

Her sheepish glances still make my stomach flutter. Bile rises up suddenly. I swallow it back down. Next, an icepick pain crawls up through my spine and flashes through my head. I hunch over and dig the heels of my hands into my eyes. I sip shallow breaths to bear the pain.

My implanted life was triggered.

Against the back of my eyelids, I see a serene meadow.

I want to look for her. This is our place. We don't think there is surveillance there. We sneak kisses here and go as far as we like in the high grass.

I want to look for her, for solace, for reassurance that everything is only a bad dream.

"Welcome to the healing center, can you open your eyes?"

Not a bad dream.

"I know you're a little sleepy right now, but can you open your eyes?"

The meadow vanishes. She vanishes. I won't get to tell her what happened. I won't be back. If I'm back, as a ghost, perhaps, my memories of her, of us, fragmented or erased.

Maybe I, too, will choose to do what Mama did after they broke her in the healing center.

My brother had stood to the side after opening the door.

Two men entered the apartment, two more men stayed by the door.

"We would very much like to invite you," the men said. "We received a report. We would like to clarify some things."

"And while you're there, maybe you make up your mind and become a Two," my brother said but looked away. "Imagine. You could earn like a Two. You don't have to be a Three. Imagine…"

I open my eyes in a sterile room. A nurse, an enviable One, in front of me, saccharine smile. They gave me something. I don't have the energy to fight.

I come to, dizzy. This is now…

This is now: I am sitting at a table at the tea shop in my hometown. And Briar is holding my hand. *In public!* I flinch before I remember that that fear is part of my implanted life. No need to fear in the present.

I need another few breaths before I am able to speak.

"That was my first flashback in public, outside the Historian-Witness Institute. Does that answer your question?"

I try to smile. I'm still in a memory of pain. Briar strokes my hand.

"Rookie."

Her sweet teasing is refreshing. People tend to encounter me with a solemn air these days when they see the Historian-Witness symbol I wear.

"Seriously. The others can have a flash without batting an eye. I nearly faint every time."

It's good to admit the inconvenient realities of my new life.

"Is it bad? Are you okay now? Anything I can do?"

"I'm okay. It can be bad, but I chose it freely."

We both look down at our hands, intertwined on the table. We take our hands back to ourselves.

"I think you chose the right path for you, Ce. I'm proud of you."

"What about you? What are you doing these days?"

"I explored a lot. I worked on the farms for a while after you first left. I got curious about preparing food, so I learned about nutrition and cooking. These days I cook and teach about cooking, and still work with the farms, too."

"That really suits you," I say.

"I agree."

"Catching or falling?" I ask. We're more mature. It's not a sore question anymore.

"Catching," Briar says. "I'm feeling a little tender today."

I revel in the present for another moment, then excuse myself. I need to prepare for the ceremony tonight.

On Remembrance Eve, five years ago, I went to the amphitheater in the grove after quarreling with Briar at the tea shop. I was hoping to meet my friend Sound there, to vent about Briar, to talk about Mary, to fret about the future. Sound was busy laying out solar panels in patches of sunlight to charge batteries for string lights.

"Need help?"

"No."

"Let me rephrase that: I need a distraction. Do you have something productive I could do?"

"Why do you need a distraction?"

"I miss Mary. And I had a fight with Briar. Again."

"There are boxes with cables. Untangle them. Someone not-me packed them up last time."

"Thank you."

"I would have been a Four," Sound said, out of nowhere.

"Don't say that…"

"I would have been a Four," he repeated, while checking a diagram on his Tab. "My skin, add one, my brain, add two. You would have been a Two, I think: you like Briar, add one. You could have checked yourself into a healing center to become a One. Or you could have made good money delivering me to a healing center."

"Sound! Why are you saying that?"

"Because it's Remembrance Eve and that's what we remember. I sometimes play 'what if' to remember."

"I would never ever have done that. Never."

"Money, though. It was powerful. If there was no other way to stay in money, you would have."

"Fuck you," I hissed and turned to leave. It was a raw and awful day. I was at my worst. Best to wait it out at home.

"Hey, Ce," Sound called me back. "I love you."

I nearly choked. Sound managed to drive a point right in between my ribs. I turned around to him.

"I love you, too. And you are right. I would have been a Two. And there's no telling what a person would do when circumstances are dire and pressure is unbearable. You've made me extremely uncomfortable just now."

"I did," Sound confirmed. "It's Remembrance. It's not supposed to be comfortable. Now untangle the cables?"

I returned to the amphitheater in the late afternoon. People were starting to gather.

I skimmed the crowd for Briar in order to avoid her. The chatter quieted when the Witness arrived. Her presence brought back memories. She had spent many months in our town, recording Mary's life. Mary and the Witness had a special bond. No wonder. To Mary, speaking to the Witness was a little like catching up with an old friend from elementary school.

"Do you think someone will volunteer to carry my life one day?" Mary asked the Witness once.

"It's possible, if you want it," the Witness replied.

What the Witness didn't say – what I read in the worry lines on her face – was that there were many more memories in the archives than Witness-candidates willing to live with them.

As darkness fell in the grove, people settled down on the sloping tiers, lit by the string lights Sound and I had hung. I spotted Briar among the group of first-timers in the first row. She was older than they were, but just as solemn.

The Witness greeted us. She told us about her journey, her decision to become a Witness. She spoke of the pain and how the implanted life sometimes disrupted her present life. She spoke of how the implanted memories shaped her perception, how the suffering had become so deeply entangled with her own soul that the urge to ease suffering had become her life's driving force.

Eventually, the Witness opened her case.

The first-timers received their memory capsules first.

When I was their age, sixteen, falling on Remembrance Eve was the trendy thing to do. I went along with all my classmates, motivated more by the fact that everyone in my class was doing it than by the symbolic weight of the act. I went along.

'I might have gone along,' I thought as I followed the line of people to the front of the amphitheater where I received my memory capsule from the Witness.

"Lest we forget, rest where we are, steer where we go," the Witness recited.

Once everyone had returned to their seats, silence settled. We swallowed our memories.

Almost immediately, reality swam in front of my eyes. Another reality took over. I felt myself inside a different body. I felt a different heart pounding in my chest. For the first time in my years of falling, I felt a different language. I startled, but then forgot myself.

Angry. Scared. Caught in sticky mud. Can't feel my legs for cold. I'm trying to move but my body is a disobedient lump of meat. I can't see well. Cracked glass shields my eyes. My hand meets a hose where my mouth should be.

"Leith!" My scream arrives in my own ears muffled.

A fog specter is blown aside and reveals a machine, not too far ahead. A two-legged terrain android. Its search beam is skimming the muddy ground in front of it.

My icy hands in unwieldy gloves fiddle with my radio. I can't find the right frequency.

"Stay still, it's looking for you," I yelp, unsure if my partner can even hear me.

"Briar," I hear his voice, all wrong and croaky. "It's here. I see it. Get away. Leave."

"No way!"

I shouldn't be going toward the thing, but I try. A blast whacks me and I stumble into the mud again.

The radio is silent. The world is silent. A thin whining sound starts up in my ears. An impact nearby. I scramble to get up. My arm suddenly feels warm and tingly.

"Leith," I scream, hear nothing anymore, remember the android, remember the radio. I look up, just in time to see the android fire once; clean, efficient, merciless. Silence.

No. I fight against the mud, my heavy legs, my bleeding arm; if there are tears, they are of rage.

"I'm going to kill you!" I start toward the war machine. It turns with a swift, nimble movement. It scans, recognizes me as enemy, and comes toward me.

So what? Let it. I have nothing to lose. I'm going to take revenge. I will cause damage.

I grope for my weapon, but my dangling arm won't support it. I'm going to tear it apart with my one bare hand, then. The mud pulls me down again. I fall. I see rolling clouds of fog, no, gas. The faceless cranium of the android appears above me.

Static in the air.

I can sense the future.

I am one with the war.

There will never be anything else.

I turn away when it shoots. It misses.

But my oxygen hose...

The toxin hits my lungs.

So I'll die. So what.

I came to, screaming, coughing, choking until I threw up. My body spasmed so much I thought I would suffocate, not on toxic gas, but on fresh forest air. A catcher was with me immediately, held me until my screams became whimpers and my heart stopped skipping over itself. Cared for by the catcher, I lay curled up in the forest amphitheater of our still, peaceful town on our verdant planet, in pain.

"Witness," I croaked and groped for the hem of her robe when I perceived her passing near me. The Witness stopped and knelt next to me. Her touch was cool against my feverish forehead, *someone's touch was cool against my burnt wrist.*

"Xe's alive! Get the tube in! Med evac! Sedate xer..."

"Ce," *the field medic,* the Witness called, "you're back."

I stared up at the Witnesses' face. I could barely believe *that I* – that Briar was alive.

"I want to become a Witness."

The toxin. Impossibly painful to speak.

"Rest now, Ce," the Witness said. "Take your time. Let's speak tomorrow."

But even a night of pain and nightmares didn't change my mind.

I dragged myself to the Witness in the morning.

I told her about my fear of forgetting, my fear of becoming complacent in peace; my regret that I had been unable to relate to Briar, unable to acknowledge that for her the past wasn't as abstract as it was for me.

The Witness invited me to the Historian-Witness Institute for a series of conversations. Nothing deterred me. I left and committed myself to becoming a Witness.

This is now: I arrive at the amphitheater. I joyfully greet Sound, still in charge of tech on Remembrance Eve. I set down the case with the memories, chosen from the archives of the Historian-Witness Institute. They are all short moments, crucial turning points, never much longer than fifteen minutes of somebody's life, though those fifteen minutes changed that life completely. We choose the moments from our records, extrapolate an immersive experience, and interlace it with a psychoactive substance to create the hallucination.

The first-timers are fidgety. I reassure them. They know what's ahead. They've taken history classes. Each chose to be here.

The crowd settles.

I tell them about my journey of the past five years. Moving to the Historian-Witness Institute. The procedure. Weeks of debilitating disorientation and panic, until I learned to tell apart the past self and myself. I had to relearn to bear the sight of a peaceful landscape. I had to work hard on feeling at ease with a stranger in the room. Peace and safety and trust seemed at odds with memories of coercion and despair in my head. After the initial healing, I undertook months of research to truly understand the memories of the implanted life: the distrust, the punishments, the healing center, the disappearances of friends and what they signified.

I close my story by reciting the Remembrance greeting.

"Lest we forget, rest where we are, steer where we go."

The crowd responds in a murmur. I distribute memories to all those who have chosen to fall. I take my seat at the center of the stage, symbolically watching over my friends as one of their catchers, as they take their memories and fall into a few minutes from another person's life.

I wake up after twelve hours of exhausted sleep. This is now. It's Remembrance Day morning. On my Tab I see a message from Briar, on a message-thread that's been silent for over five years.

Tea shop for breakfast, if you're not busy?

Yes please. Give me an hour.

It takes me a while to get ready after sleeping. My mind lets go in sleep. Memories get tangled up, especially after intense days, such as giving a Remembrance Eve ceremony in my hometown, where I decided to become a Witness, where I abandoned my girlfriend, overwhelmed by her memories.

I check in with my Witness mentor. I meditate. I honor my implanted memories. I remind myself of what is now and what is past.

Finally, I set out into the brilliant morning to meet Briar at the tea vendor's shop.

"Rest where we are," the tea vendor greets us.

"Steer where we go," we respond.

Yan assesses us through half-closed eyes. We're safe to allow xer to see us. Xer scales move into equilibrium. The space fills with warm scents of roasting spices, steam meanders through the air. Yan puts two blueberry scones on plates.

Briar and I find a shaded table under an awning. We're having tea and scones on Remembrance Day morning. This is now.

"Would you tell me about how you snuck me your memory back then?" I ask.

"I liked you. A lot. You were used to talking to Mary. Mary shared difficult memories with you often. But I wasn't Mary. I couldn't do it. I wanted you to know about me. But I couldn't tell the story. So I asked Mary's Witness for help. She extracted the memory and she gave it to you that night, because I asked her to. Because I wanted you to know."

"Do you have many more memories like that?"

"I was in the war three years."

"What were you hoping for when you gave me that moment?"

"For us to work out despite the stuff I couldn't talk about."

"And I ran away and didn't speak to you for five years."

"Yea," she sighs. "I was angry at you. I felt vindicated at times. You really couldn't take it, I thought, even though you seemed obsessed with that whole Remembrance thing, obsessed with Mary and primaries, your culture's past. I thought you were cynical, too. All of you. I thought, 'you exploit your ancestors for their hardships to sustain peace and equality. Must you do that? Can't you keep peace without using someone's pain?'"

I place my hand on Briar's arm softly to wordlessly ask her for patience. I need a moment to think.

"I was afraid," I say, "and still am afraid, that oppression is an addiction that will never be overcome. So, out of caution, I prefer to be vigilant and do the work of witnessing the past in the way I chose. I would not force this way on anyone else. I'm wary when I work with a community where there seems to be cultural pressure to fall on Remembrance Eve. I don't want people to feel pressured to fall. There are other ways to engage with the past. There are important ways to engage with the present, too, ways to think ahead to the future. I can articulate that now.

"And I understand that somebody may call these practices exploiting our ancestors. I see it as honoring our ancestors. When you first arrived here, I was working with Mary and her Witness every day. You're right: I was preoccupied with our past and I was used to Mary sharing difficult memories openly. I honestly didn't realize that you are a primary, too."

Briar takes a bite of her scone. We would never have been able to disagree about complicated topics so calmly five years ago, but this is now.

"Ce, I'd most like to be called a person," Briar says. "Not 'primary.' Not 'witness,' not 'survivor.' I'd like to just be a person."

"I get it. I'm sorry, Briar."

"Do you think you might consider sticking around?"

This is now, I remind myself. Tea and blueberry scones with Briar on a lovely spring morning, at odds with her past, my implanted past, our past. But this is now.

"I wouldn't mind coming back."

Anna Ziegelhof is a horror and science fiction writer residing in the San Francisco Bay Area. A former academic with a subject background in Sociology, she is drawn to philosophical stories with sparks of hope and whimsy, featuring themes such as identity, memory, and belonging. Her short fiction can be found, among others, in *The Horror Library, Luna Station, Solarpunk Magazine, The Future Fire, Daily Science Fiction,* and *Flametree Press.* When she isn't writing, she enjoys encountering strange places, being in nature, and looking at art. Online she can be found at www.annaziegelhof.com

All You Ever Wanted

Jamie M Boyd

My daughter glared. "But what if there's a car crash? Or a plane crash? Or a fire?" What if I get some rare, incurable cancer? Are you saying you want me to die? *Permanently?*"

I forced my expression to stay cool. I'd spent most of Rebecca's life drilling into her the dangers posed by the outside world. But never in those seventeen years did I anticipate my own vigilance being turned against me – for her to come running into our tiny kitchen, excited as a toddler with a new toy, to say she wanted to tear her beautiful brain apart, nanoslice by nanoslice, to upload into an immortal, digital form.

I'm proud to say I didn't flinch. Instead, I put down the dishrag and channeled the voice of thousands of mothers who came before me, echoing down the millennia in shared solidarity against the breathtaking foolishness of teenagers.

"Absolutely not," I said. "Over my dead body."

The arch of her brow suggested this, too, could be arranged. She opened her mouth to protest, then stopped cold and shrugged. The casualness of the gesture was more frightening than any tantrum she could throw, any argument she could devise. Her brown eyes narrowed.

"Just wait until I'm twenty-one."

I told myself it was just a childish threat, something she'd grow out of. It was easier for me to think that way than to consider her desire inevitable – my fault, even. I was the one who first insisted on the nightly back-ups.

Rebecca was five. The year, 2032. The cost: more than I could afford on a nurse's salary. I didn't care. Fifteen years working nights in a Florida emergency room had taught me all I needed to know about the fragility of life. I was ready to buy whatever they were selling.

The surgeons put the recording device right at her nape, by her hairline, just like in the infomercials. David was against it, but it'd been so long since he'd taken an interest in anything to do with parenting, his wishes were easy enough for me to ignore. Since the divorce, my daughter was all I had left.

Afterward, Rebecca assured me that it didn't hurt, and I slept better knowing that if she was ever seriously injured or worse (the ads never explicitly mentioned death, but it was strongly implied in the slow-motion freeze of the camera right before the girl stepped out into traffic) that there would be a copy of her brain scans safe and sound in the computer.

True, the MirrorMe representatives made no guarantees about what could be done with those crude copies. (Turned out, not much. Technology, after all, was not as advanced back then.) But everyone had a sense of breakthroughs just around the corner.

One month after Rebecca's surgery, paramedics dragged the Morales boy from the bottom of his swimming pool down the street. One look at his mother's face, and I knew I'd made the right choice.

Sometimes I blame the U.S. government. The real problems with Rebecca started after they closed the schools. The physical ones, I mean.

They sold it as a safety measure, after all the mass shootings and pandemics. Parents shouldn't have to kiss their children goodbye in the morning and wonder if they'll ever see them again – or if they'll bring home a plague. So instead of climbing into a yellow school bus, Rebecca slid into a large, school board-issued pod that sat in the corner of her bedroom gleaming like a silver, egg-shaped mirror.

Three decades of budget cuts meant the campuses were crumbling and all but the most devoted or desperate teachers had already quit. The last few dutifully pointed out the bugs in the AI that replaced them, and superintendents congratulated themselves on engineering the perfect employee – one that could be endlessly replicated to teach thousands of children, one that didn't need sleep or medical benefits.

Rebecca loved it. I had to coax her out of the pod at the end of the school day, bribing her with fresh-baked cookies and promises of upgraded skins to keep her from diving right back into a world where she could sing colors and dance in storms of quadratic equations. Her grades skyrocketed, but I wasn't so sure I liked the other changes. She was jittery and distracted – impatient with the world and, above all, with me.

The new school or just hormones? I needed to see for myself.

"This place makes me nauseous," I grumbled as I attended Parkside Middle's Open House Night.

I'd squeezed my body into my daughter's pod, and my eyes were still adjusting to the virtual classroom. About two dozen ordinary-looking desks filled with parent avatars sat on a dim desert landscape. Above gaped a night sky strewn with stars and zipping comets, a field so vast it would have made me dizzy even in reality. But that wasn't what bothered me.

What bothered me was the teacher who stood at the front of the desks and whose appearance kept changing during the welcome presentation – from a nostalgic, 1950s schoolmarm with cat-eye glasses to a 6-foot-tall fluorescent blue Tyrannosaurus Rex, to a bald, androgynous Kung Fu master floating two feet off the ground in the lotus position.

"Studies have shown that by tailoring my appearance to dovetail with your children's interests, I can hold their attention longer and be a more effective instructor," the floating Kung Fu master said with a wise smile before they flickered and became a pink octopus with writhing tentacles. "Of course, I don't really think of myself as a teacher. I'm more of a friend and tour guide."

When the octopus began juggling a skateboard, a seashell, and spinning globe of Earth, I shot an uneasy look at the father crammed into the desk beside mine.

"You buying this?" I whispered to him.

Or at least, that's what I tried to ask. Back in the pod, my mouth moved. In the classroom, however, my avatar froze, and the words went unspoken.

"So sorry," interrupted the teacher/tour guide/now-dinosaur, gesturing with his tiny blue arms. "Students are not allowed to talk to other students during instructional time, and right now, the program is reading you both as students."

I blinked. "What about socialization?" I asked, careful to direct the question to the teacher.

"We found it was necessary to limit because of bullying. Suicides have fallen forty-two percent district-wide since the change. We've also seen a drop in eating disorders, binge drinking and general depression. I'm sure you want to spare your daughter all that."

Suicide? I thought back to my own middle and high school years: the acne and braces and the never-ending anxiety. The taunts and months of eating lunch alone. It had been bad, but surely not that bad. I knew Rebecca struggled after the divorce, and she never brought friends over anymore, but I figured that was because everything was online now. I'd know it if something was really wrong, if she was really unhappy, wouldn't I?

I swallowed, then nodded slowly in agreement with the teacher.

I can't really blame Tsakhiagiin Chenghiz, although I'd like to. He was a bioengineering student from Mongolia. And Rebecca was in love.

"He wants to meet you," Rebecca said as we sat down for brunch at my favorite café. She'd just turned nineteen. "He's very traditional. In his culture, it's custom to ask the parent first, for permission to get married."

"Married?" I gaped as our drinks arrived. "But you're so— You haven't even finished college yet. Has he secured a job? Did he get a work visa?"

Rebecca stared at me. "No, Mom. I told you. He *lives* in Mongolia. He wants to meet you in the Verse. That's where we met."

I frowned. She was always in the Verse.

Even now. She held up a finger and flicked her eyes off to a point in the distance, so I knew she was accepting an incoming message from a friend there, thanks to those damn cortical implants. While I waited, I glanced around the mostly empty restaurant, stomach churning. This place used to be packed on Sundays. It wasn't hard to guess where everyone was.

Even my Luddite friends worked in the Verse now. I was thankful my job at the hospital was one of the few that still required in-person contact. Rebecca liked to accuse me of being anti-technology, but that wasn't it. How can you heal someone, comfort someone, if you can't hold their hand?

I reached for my daughter across the table, hoping to recapture her attention.

She ended her other conversation and smiled. "Cheng says hello. And don't worry, you'll adore him. The Verse will translate for you both."

"He doesn't speak English?" I blurted. "Why not?"

Rebecca's face hardened. "I don't know, Mom. Why don't *you* speak Mongolian?"

I blushed, and an awkward silence fell as the waitress came to take our order. When she left, I tried again: "So, uh, you're following him over there, then? What about getting your master's? And is it really safe traveling now, with all the bombings?"

Rebecca cocked her head, bewildered. "No one's moving anywhere."

"But you just said you're getting married."

"Yeah?"

"So how can you be married with an ocean between you?"

Rebecca laughed with a coy, almost embarrassed smile that hinted at technology I didn't want to think about. She shook her head.

"Oh, Mom. You're so old fashioned."

Believe it or not, I don't fault my ex. God knows how, but David managed to convince Rebecca not to rush into anything once she turned the legal upload age of twenty-one. (Of course, she listened to *him.* Daughters really know how to twist the knife.)

Although she got her own apartment, she rarely left her pod. I tried visiting her in the Verse a dozen or so times, but apparently, I'm also among the two percent of people for whom the sense of vertigo there never goes away. It was like a funhouse with endless rooms, where the laws of physics didn't apply. Every time, I had to leave to avoid throwing up.

To keep in touch, we resorted to using outdated technology, instant messaging once a week. Years passed, and even those messages tapered off.

Helen@Beccasmom_gmail: It's been seven years since you married. Where are my grandbabies?

Rebecca011235813_verse: <sigh> i told you cheng and i don't believe in biological reproduction it's not ethically responsible

Helen@Beccasmom_gmail: How can you be so naive?

Rebecca011235813_verse: plus u alrdy have a grandchild in the verse ... ari is there for u to get to know anytime u deem her worthy of yr attention shed love to meet u.

Helen@Beccasmom_gmail: A computer simulation is not a child.

Rebecca011235813_verse: did u get anti-nausea pills i sent? give hr a chance...

Helen@Beccasmom_gmail: I'm sure I'd love her. That's what I'm afraid of.

Rebecca011235813_verse: that dsnt make any sense

Helen@Beccasmom_gmail: I already spend half my day talking to Alexa and Godfrey. Even my Roomba, for Christ sake. If you fill your life with artificial intelligence, where is there any room left for people?

Rebecca011235813_verse: did u just compare my child to a vacuum

Helen@Beccasmom_gmail: I didn't mean it that way.

Rebecca011235813_verse: dad loves her ... he says shes a wonder

Helen@Beccasmom_gmail: Of course he does. Automated grand-parenting sounds right up his alley.

Rebecca011235813_verse: at least hes making an effort

Helen@Beccasmom_gmail: And what have I been doing since you were born?

Rebecca011235813_verse: <eyeroll emoji> r we really doing this *again*

Helen@Beccasmom_gmail: Yes. You can't just ignore me. I'm not one of your programs.

Rebecca011235813_verse: wtv if u want to have a real conversation u know where to find us

<Rebecca011235813_verse has terminated this session.>

There was a knock on my door. An *actual* knock on the *actual* door.

I stood and answered it, with the help of my new bionic knees. It was Rebecca, in the flesh. Although we still messaged dutifully each month (careful to stick to safe topics that wouldn't trigger a fight), it'd been three years since I'd seen my daughter's body. I was startled by the middle-age softness developing around her belly and upper arms, which her Verseion didn't reflect. I drank in her scent, another thing the virtual world didn't recreate, musky with a hint of apricot.

Panic filled me as I suddenly understood the reason for her visit. "I won't let you do it!"

Rebecca pushed her way in and laughed. "Not your choice anymore. Hasn't been for a long time."

I wracked my brain for any lever I could pull to stop this. "I'm the old-timer. Shouldn't you be trying to convince me to upload? Why don't you let me be the guinea pig, and you worry about yourself later, when they've got all the transfer protocols sorted out a little better?"

"They sorted it out years ago, Mom. Thousands of people have already shifted. Tens of thousands. All successfully."

My eyes narrowed. "You think they make the failures public? You can't complain once you're dead. And your digital copy won't know the difference. Honey, if they lose even half a percent of your memories—"

"Who is this evil 'they' you're imagining, Mom? My company's been upgrading the software for the past five years. It's my code."

"Then come up with a better way of scanning living tissue, instead of this ... butchery. That way you don't have to choose between life here and there. You could have both."

"I don't want both."

I froze, thunderstruck. All I could think was: That day, when she was seven, and I caught her climbing the towering oak tree at the park? I should've told her to climb *higher*. I should've bought her that giant trampoline she asked for three Christmases in a row, screw what it would've done to my insurance premiums. I should've taught her to drive instead of relying on autopilot. And that night she wanted to ride downtown with her friends to see that awful band in that sketchy bar? I should've told her to stay out late, dance all night, kiss too many boys (or girls). No. I should have told her to get really, really stoned.

Rebecca, who had done none of these things, smiled gently. "If it makes you feel better, I would have uploaded ages ago if it wasn't for you. I kept thinking I could change your mind, bring you with us. Then you had the surgery for your knees, and I finally realized. You're never going to let your body go."

I stayed silent a long time, tasting bile. "What would your father say?"

My ex-husband had been dead three years. Heart attack, no backup. His funeral had been the last time I'd seen Rebecca in person.

She shook her head. "He'd probably try to convince me to stay, then acknowledge that it was ultimately my choice to make." She put her hand over mine. "The way he made his."

My body trembled. "I'll be alone. You're doing this to punish me."

Rebecca pinched her fingers to the bridge of her nose, then let them fall. "No. I'm doing this because I want to be with my husband. I want to be with my child. *Forever*. If nothing else, you can at least understand that."

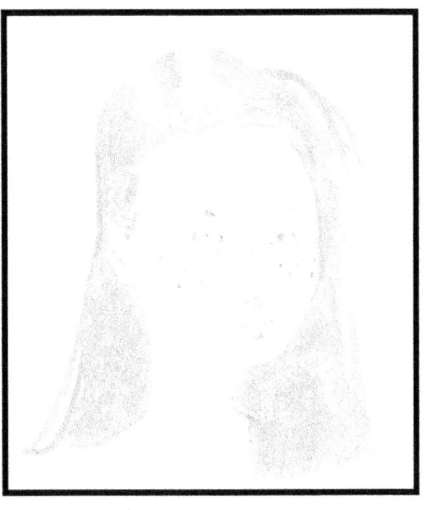

I looked down at my hands, blinking away tears. I could, but I'd never admit it. Rebecca knew this and took me into her arms. The sensation was warm and strange and wonderful, already an artifact from another era.

"Think of it this way," Rebecca whispered. "I'll be safe. Always. Wasn't that all you ever wanted?"

And that was the saddest thing. It had been.

Jamie M. Boyd is a writer and former journalist from Florida. Her short fiction has appeared in *Strange Horizons, Heartlines Spec, Mysterion,* and *Luna Station Quarterly*. As a reporter, she was part of a newspaper staff twice named finalist for the Pulitzer Prize. Find her at jamiemboyd.com or on Bluesky @jamieboyd.

You think it's a coincidence that this same poster is on every south-facing corner between here and what you think is your mother's house? *Past* the house where the dogs bark a little too loud. The comfort place. Safety. Catch up with the old woman, learn the neighborhood gossip. Get a piece of pie or pineapple upside-down cake, freshly baked. And you're brightening *her* day, right?

You think it's a coincidence this same message is also in your facebook stream, links to it on twitter, instagram. Do you think it's a little strange, after the direction things went for so long? Heightened tensions, embargoes. Bad things in the works. And then – what – regime change? You really think the right and the left are so different, that the world changes like that – no growing pains, no struggle?

The great World Religion Conference. All that kumbaya'ing and popes and rajas and Sunnis clapping each other on the back. Everything got nice. Got very nice. The bad-dream-of-a-president long gone.

Well, listen up. I'm only going to say it once. The path the world was careening through space at – a path of world war and climate change disaster, tsunamis and cyber bullying, presidents shooting randos in the street – it happened. Bullseye. Slam dunk. Not even any net.

Don't listen to me if I tell you the world is gone. I don't know that. Just because everybody I knew in life is gone, doesn't mean there's not more out there. The infrastructure, you see, is gone. I'm a woman, like you. Hunkered in an experimental franchised VR medical facility made for quadriplegics to walk and talk in their minds, and I'm watching you. Poring over you like you're a Petri dish, a terrarium. Keeping you safe, like a baby, swaddled in delusion.

If you're reading this, you should know: Randy says we're done. The power will be kaput before the end of the week. All this niceness – the thoughtful boyfriend, your clean bill of health, that perfect nose of yours, *friends* – all of that is about to close like a browser window.

I want you to know that it was never a chore. It was a job I loved, a thing I did because I wanted the world to grow straight, to be strong. To be filled with love and peace and happy endings.

But there's a real, honest-to-God pack of wolves out here, and it's time to move on. Get on your feet and come if you can.

Yeah You, Come Here

Douglas Gwilym

Bram Stoker Award nominated short-story author **Douglas Gwilym** has been known to compose a weird-fiction rock opera or two. He co-edits *The Midnight Zone*, reads classics of the proto-Weird on YouTube, and makes games with his daughter. Stories at *Penumbric, LampLight, Lucent Dreaming, Tales from the Moonlit Path,* and *Tales to Terrify.*

These Quiet Constellations

M Shedric Simpson

"Sometimes you hear the stars themselves speaking," Andra said, his words floating somewhere behind Basit's right shoulder. "Like a whisper, in a language all their own."

He pivoted away, leaving Basit to the rumble of the ocean and the laughter of the teenagers circled around him. The wind was cold on Basit's bare back. He glanced around nervously, but couldn't make out anyone's expressions in the scant moonlight.

Tori stepped towards him. "Are you ready?"

"What do I have to do?"

"Just relax. We'll take care of everything," Tori said. "You brought one?"

Basit reached into his bag and pulled out the enneakra. It wriggled beneath his touch – a nine-limbed star, golden and softly furred. Wire-thin tendrils slid out of puckered orifices, probing, then retreated back into the creature's body. Basit had found it on the beach just before sunset.

Tori took the enneakra. "You know there's no going back, right? This will change you forever."

Basit nodded, his tongue numb. He tried to keep his eyes away from Tori's left hand, and the stubs where her pinky and ring finger should have been.

"Swear you'll never tell anyone," Tori said. Her eyes blazed in the darkness. "Not even your parents. Not till there's so many of us that the Confederacy can't stop us."

"I won't tell anyone," Basit said. His chest tightened. "Not ever."

"Good. Andra said we could trust you." She caught Basit by the shoulder and turned him around, until he was facing out toward the waves and the darkness. "Let's do this."

The other teenagers moved closer, every one of them at least a year older than Basit. It felt like an initiation. Like he was becoming one of them. But he honestly didn't care what any of them thought. He just wanted to be closer to Andra. It was all he'd wanted since Andra and Tori had arrived with their parents last year. The thought of sharing something sacred and secret with Andra sent a thrill running through his entire body.

He felt a hand on the small of his back, painting his skin with something slick and cold as the sea. It smelled like the rotten things the tides cast up along the shore. "This'll trick the enneakra into bonding with you," Tori said. "Are you ready?"

Basit nodded. He didn't trust himself to speak. His eyes met with Andra's, standing a few feet away, and for a moment they shared a secret smile.

"Do it," Tori said.

A moment later Basit felt the enneakra against his skin. He held his breath, not knowing what to expect. It wriggled against his spine, small and wet and unfamiliar, but nothing seemed different. Then the enneakra's tendrils pierced his skin like a hundred needles full of fire.

Basit's body convulsed. He would have screamed if his lungs had functioned. He dropped to his knees, jaw clenched against the pain. A hand grasped his shoulder.

"It's okay," Tori said. "That's the worst of it."

He grunted in response. Andra knelt at his left side. "You did great," he said.

"We're going to change the world," Tori said. "We're going to make a world without lies. A world where no one's ever a stranger. And you're going to be a part of it."

"Mmhmm."

"Drink lots of water. The enneakra needs the moisture. It'll take about a day to bond with your nervous system. We'll talk again after that. For now just take it easy, and remember not to tell anyone."

"I won't." Basit finally managed to wrangle control of his voice.

"Good." Tori squeezed Basit's shoulder again. "We gotta get home before it gets too late. See you tomorrow." Her footsteps receded in the sand, along with those of the other teenagers, and for a moment he was alone with Andra on the beach.

Andra's lips brushed against Basit's cheek. "Tomorrow," he said, and it sang like a promise in Basit's ear.

The world changed overnight.

Basit woke from dreams of reaching out to Andra, of clasping hands across the sky, and of breath joined as one. Vibrant and immense, and far more vivid than the breakfast packet his mother had left on the counter for him before retreating to her office.

He stumbled through his lessons. Strange sensations bubbled within his thoughts – explosions of joy and frustration like distant fireworks. Not his own feelings, yet he was aware of them just the same. Trying to focus on trigonometry and xenobotanical classification was all but impossible when all he wanted to do was listen for Andra's voice amongst the others.

He slipped out of the house the first moment he could, carrying two seaplums in the pocket of his windbreaker. The bay lay before him, cobalt blue and restless beneath a windswept sky. Waves crashed against the polycrete jetties that surrounded the algae fields, sending clouds of foam into the air. Massive harvesters shuffled like mammoths in the space between.

"Hey."

Basit turned at the sound of Andra's voice. He couldn't help smiling at the sight of his dark hair tumbling in the wind. "Hey."

"I felt it last night. You thinking about me." Andra laughed. "I think the whole village felt it."

"Oh." Basit's skin burned. He reached for the small of his back, as if covering up the enneakra could hide his emotions. "I, uh—"

"It's okay. It takes a while to get the hang of. To learn how to whisper instead of shouting."

He blushed harder, fighting the urge to turn away. "I could feel you too, I think. It was – I don't even know how to describe it."

"That's the point. You don't have to anymore." And he was right. Basit could feel the sincerity behind Andra's words. A warm glow wrapped around each thought.

"Yeah. It's magical."

Andra nodded to the dark rocks along the beach, north of the algae fields. "You wanted to walk?"

"Yeah." Basit fumbled at his pocket. "I brought you a plum."

"You're sweet."

He handed one to Andra, then took the other for himself. Andra took a bite, then wiped the juice from his chin. Basit had to tear his eyes away from Andra's lips. They fell into step alongside each other, silent while they finished eating. The little village and its prefabs fell away behind them, until all that surrounded them were the dusky green hills to their left and the restless sea to their right. The sand and pebbles gave way to rugged black stone scaled with patches of pinkish mollusks. A few enneakra crept like errant stars across the rocks, looking for nourishment or whatever it was that sent them journeying endlessly across the beaches.

"What Tori said about changing the world, was that true?"

"She means it." Andra tossed the plum pit out into the waves, then wiped his hands on his shorts. "She wants to take down the Confederacy. If it weren't for the Confederacy, my family would still be back on Vondal's World, instead of here in the middle of nowhere."

"Oh." Basit bit his lip. "I'm sorry."

Andra turned his head sideways. "It's not all bad, you know." He raised an eyebrow. "Being out here."

Basit was sure Andra was teasing, but he felt the color of Andra's words through the enneakra. Some of the tension melted out of his jaw. "Will you ever go back?"

"Probably not." Andra shrugged. "Mom would. But not Dad or Tori."

Basit hesitated. "Is it about what happened to her hand?" He knew what it meant to be an outsider. Though for him, it was just being awkward, and nothing so obvious as Tori's missing fingers.

Andra bit his lip. "Not like you're thinking. Tori was born that way. And they could have fixed it. Heck, they probably have the facilities to fix it even here. But Dad just didn't think it was right to force her into surgery."

"So he just decided for her?"

"No, that was her decision. She said she was happy the way she was." Andra sighed. "It shouldn't have been a big deal, but it's the provincial capital. Everything's political. Dad talked about her in some of his lectures at the university. Word got around, the grants dried up, and suddenly he wasn't getting any assignments. So now we're here, farming algae for a living."

"I'm sorry."

"Dad seems happier, anyway," Andra said. "I think he likes it here."

"Was Vondal's World much different?"

"Night and day. Both good, but different, you know?" Andra slipped his hand into Basit's. "Tori says the Interstellar Confederacy only cares about control. Ensuring that humanity is identical on every one of the sixty-seven worlds. That's why the fuss about her hand. So she wants to show that there's different ways of being human. To prove that the Confederacy is wrong."

Half of Andra's words washed past him. It was times like this that he recognized the difference between their pasts, yet Andra never seemed to look down on him for it. "Would the enneakra change that much?"

Andra laughed. "Well, politicians aren't gonna like a world where they can't lie anymore. But I think it's bigger than that. Our whole society will change. We'll never be alone again."

Their fingers twined and knotted. Basit's neck tingled in the breeze. "I like that idea."

"It's going to take some work. But every revolution starts somewhere." Andra shrugged. "Okay I'm dying to know. What's all the way out here? Are we just lost?"

Basit smiled. He'd been planning this for days. "Not lost. Just a little further."

They wove their way over dark rocks, pale sand, and tidal pools trapped between. Their clasped fingers spoke one language, while their enneakra whispered in another. Basit felt like a whirling planet, and the pull of Andra's heart was the gravity that bound their orbits.

"You know Mom's gonna kill me if I'm back late…"

Basit tugged him into the shadow of a looming crag, just steps from the water's edge. "It's here." The tide had been high this morning, but he needn't have worried – the house he'd built still stood. Driftwood walls and crimson seastrand curtains, tucked into a natural alcove in the rocks. Iridescent shells lined the path to the door

"You built this?"

Basit grinned, trying to make a joke of it. "Might be a little drafty, I know." He shrugged. "But like you said – gotta start somewhere."

Andra squeezed his hand. "Bas. I love it."

A warm pulse of sincerity backed Andra's words, lifting Basit out of the pool of doubt he'd been drowning in for months. For once, he didn't have to fumble for what to say. He opened his heart and let the enneakra say all the things he'd never been able to.

Basit turned, and then Andra's lips were there, pressing against his own. Bodies twined together, they stumbled to the door.

Andra pushed Basit to the ground the moment they were inside. The blankets were damp beneath Basit's back, but he didn't care. Andra dropped on top of him and their bodies moved against each other. Basit gasped as Andra's lips found his neck.

"Won't everyone see?" he managed.

"Let them." Andra's breath was hot on Basit's skin. Basit closed his eyes and reached out. The invisible thread that connected them sang with light. He felt his own heart. He felt Andra's. He felt the other teenagers in town, and the ten thousand enneakra on the beach around them. All connected, all glowing, like a constellation writ in love.

Basit woke thrashing, alone, though the scent of Andra's body still clung to his skin. A thousand moths swarmed his throat. He felt pain. He felt fear. Not his own, but Andra's. Pouring into him with the force of a two-moon tide. He threw himself out of bed, sheets sliding like rotten seaweed beneath him.

The latch on the window refused to slide. The house had already switched into night mode. He pulled out his tablet and keyed in an override. The urgency of Andra's fear surrounded him as he slipped over the sill and landed barefoot in the silken grass below.

The sky bristled with broken clouds, torn between the two moons. Andra's house was lit up beneath it, warm yellow light spilling from the windows. Basit dashed across the garden between their homes.

His mouth was numb. He tried to send his thoughts back through the enneakra, calling out to Andra to say he was on his way, but his own anxiety made it hard to focus. He took a deep breath as he came up on the house.

Tori stood beside the gnarled sitia tree in their yard. "Basit. Wait." Her face was pale – warm brown hues washed out by the cold moonlight. "You can't go in."

"What do you mean?" Basit's fear turned to anger in a flash. "Can't you feel it? Something happened to Andra!"

"I know. He's gone. But running in there's just going to make it worse."

"Gone where?"

Tori took a breath. "Inland. The sheriff took him in the shuttle."

"Why? For what?"

"I don't know how it happened exactly. I was asleep." Tori's shoulders slumped. "Andra came home late. His shirt was wet and mom spotted the enneakra under it. She freaked out, called the clinic. They said Andra needed to go to the hospital."

Guilt shot through Basit's heart like a burning needle. He was the reason Andra had come home late. "Then we have to go too. Tell them that the enneakra can't hurt him."

Tori's eyes flashed. "Did you think this was all just a game? If the IC magistrates find out about us they'll burn the whole village as post-humans. Not just you and me, but our friends and our families too. Everybody."

Basit throat tightened. He heard his voice rise "They wouldn't do that."

"Just turn on the news. They do it all the time. Make an example of some shithole little town like this one, just to keep the other worlds in line."

"Then all the more reason we have to go after Andra!"

"Don't you understand? He could have called for help, but he didn't. He let Mom think it was an accident. That no one else was involved. He was trying to protect us. To protect you."

Basit shook his head, trying to calm his thoughts enough to reach Andra through the enneakra. "We've gotta do something!"

"There's nothing we can do. The shuttle's gone. We just have to wait out the surgery, and be there for him when he comes home. We'll find another enneakra, it'll be like nothing ever happened. I promise."

"We could take the transport barge. My dad has the access codes." Basit knew how irrational he was being, but he couldn't stop himself. Andra's fear sang through his soul, and his emotions twisted like pebbles caught in the churning surf.

"Basit. Just be with him," Tori said. She settled her hands on Basit's shoulders. "Make sure he knows he's not alone."

Basit resisted for a moment, then collapsed into the hug. "I'm scared," he said.

"He's going to be okay." Tori's words were steady, yet the enneakra betrayed her fear. "Everything's gonna be all right."

But it wasn't. Even after Basit slipped back through the window and into his bed, Andra's panic followed him. He held on tight as he could, remembering every moment they'd spent together and sending those feelings. It didn't matter. An hour before dawn Andra's enneakra vanished, and all Basit was left with was a terrible silence.

Basit brought the stone down hard. Yellow blood spattered the rocks, and a needle of flame raced up Basit's spine. He clenched his jaw as the enneakra's life sputtered out. He'd killed dozens of the star-shaped monsters this morning, but it had done nothing to numb the ache inside his heart. Nothing had felt right in the two weeks since Andra had vanished.

He wanted to scream, as if that could somehow pierce through Andra's coma and wake him. But the doctors had cut them apart, and the enneakra on Basit's back sparked like an angry wire, bringing nothing but pain.

He dropped the ichor-stained rock and set off down the beach. The pebble shoal was rough beneath his feet, but kinder than the tide of what-ifs that whirled around him.

That one night beneath the driftwood sky would live inside Basit forever. The way that their lips had touched. The way that their hearts had moved in unison. Nothing would ever be that perfect again.

"Basit."

He glanced over his shoulder to find Tori following him down the beach, dressed in a windbreaker and shorts. Anger flashed through him. It wasn't right that Tori should look so calm. Not so soon after Andra had been taken away.

"We need to talk."

Basit didn't want to talk. Not to anyone. Everyone just went on, as if nothing had happened, and he hated it. "Go away."

"I know you're hurting," Tori said. "We all are."

"I'm fine, okay?"

"We can all feel your grief. You shouldn't be alone in it."

Tori just stood there, all windblown hair and rugged beauty, like the protagonist in some sim, and for a moment Basit absolutely hated her. "How is it you don't feel anything?"

"I do. We all do," Tori said. "You know that."

Basit had kept his thoughts as far from the enneakra as he could over the last two weeks. The enneakra was a wound that wouldn't scab over. Yet there was no way he could turn it off. As soon as he touched it he could sense the pain inside Tori's heart, raw and deep, a twin to his own.

It wasn't just hurt. Strands of guilt and helplessness twisted round Tori's grief. All the same feelings that had dwelt within Basit's breast, even if they were bound into different knots. He shook his head. "I'm sorry," he said at last.

Tori placed her hand in the center of Basit's chest. Two fingers and a thumb, spread wide like the limbs of an enneakra. "You're not alone. You never will be again."

"I am, though. He's gone, and it's all my fault." Basit felt something crack inside him as he finally said the words aloud. Tori's face went blurry. The world went blurry. "He might never come back."

"No. He's still here. Inside you. Inside of all of us." Reflections of the ragged sky churned in her eyes. "You just have to open yourself up. Listen."

What was there to listen to? His soul was a tempest, it was hard to see anything beyond it. He closed his eyes and reached out beyond himself.

Tori's heart beat fierce and loud, but there were others beyond. The other teenagers back in the village looked on, sympathy and friendship extended like open hands. Basit felt naked beneath their gaze, his soul laid bare. He wished he could tear the enneakra out of his flesh, but Tori had already warned him that there was no going back. His cheeks burned. He turned his face towards the ocean. He wished it were Andra standing beside him instead.

"Basit—"

Sometimes you hear the stars themselves speaking. Those were the words that Andra had told him, the night that Tori had placed the star upon his back. *Like a whisper, in a language all their own,* he'd said.

He took a breath. The electric static of the ocean washed over him; he tasted seaweed on his tongue. He felt Tori beside him. He felt the teenagers back in town. And somewhere out beyond the waves, a million points of light, warm and glimmering. But there was more than that. Somehow, Basit felt *him.* He couldn't see him, he couldn't hear his voice, yet he recognized him just the same. A piece of Andra's spirit, dancing between those quiet constellations.

"It's him. I can feel him." He reached towards the ocean. Towards the invisible light that dwelt within it.

"He's still with us." Tori put her hand on Basit's shoulder. "You're not alone. And you never will be again."

✳

Basit had lived with the ghost for so long that he barely recognized the real Andra when he finally returned.

The boy that stepped off the shuttle was thinner and quieter than Andra, and the light brown of his skin not as warm as it once had been. Like the sunlight had gone out of him, replaced with some cheap electric light.

Andra's mother swept him into a hug before he even cleared the landing pad. A moment later Tori was there too, and then Andra's father, all laughing and crying. Basit didn't know why he stood back. Joy and relief poured out of Tori's enneakra, and Basit tried to mirror it with his own, even knowing that Andra wouldn't feel anything. Couldn't feel anything. That part of him had been cut away.

They shuffled back to Andra's house as a mob, nearly half the village milling around with Andra at the center. Andra's mother handed out drinks while everyone bubbled about just how wonderful it was to have him back. The enneakra whispered amongst each other, a tangle of hope and worry and gratitude invisible to the adults in the room.

Andra nodded and shook hands until the house was almost empty again. Until the two of them were alone in the dining room, with just a few feet of synthetic grey carpet between them.

"I missed you," Basit said. The words didn't seem enough, not without the earnestness of the enneakra behind them. "I missed

you so much."

Andra avoided his gaze, saying nothing. He looked exhausted and quiet in a way that Basit never remembered seeing.

"It must have been a long day – the flight and everything." He just wanted everything to go back to the way it'd been eight months earlier, when spring had been filled with promise and Andra's breath had been hot on his neck.

"Mmhm."

"Maybe we could meet up tomorrow? Go for a walk?"

Andra shrugged. "Tomorrow."

Basit took a half step back. "Okay." He'd almost forgotten what it was like to try to talk without the enneakra. Without understanding what the words someone said really meant. It was like trying to talk to his mother. "I'll see you then."

Andra's words stopped him halfway through the door. "You could have written," he said.

"What?"

"You could have written. Sent a video. Anything."

"You were in a coma."

"Yeah." Andra's voice soured. "I was."

"We were all hoping you'd come home."

"Then why did you forget me?" Andra asked. "Why did I wake up alone, without as much as a letter? I spent three weeks in rehab, and every day of it was agony, and every day of it was alone."

"None of us even knew you were awake until this morning!"

"You had eight months to write. Eight months."

Except Basit had been with Andra every minute. Listening to the shimmer of his spirit as it leapt along the horizon. Sending love and hoping Andra would feel it. "I was thinking of you the whole time."

"Yeah? Well you sure didn't say anything."

"I'm sorry! It's just—" Basit reached out, but Andra was already halfway up the stairs, not bothering to look back.

The voices from the kitchen fell away, and Basit dropped his hand back to his waist. Silence whirled around him like a rising tide, until the weight of it was enough to drown.

They gathered on the beach the next night, a mile north of the village. Far enough to escape the prying eyes of the adults. There were more of them now – almost twenty – and Eve had taken Basit's place as the youngest. Just like eight months earlier, but played in reverse. Now Basit stood with the others in the circle, and Andra was the one alone in the center. Ripples of anticipation danced between their enneakra. Maybe Basit's anxiety was contagious. Or maybe all of them felt that way. When they stood so close it was hard to tell.

The enneakra would fix everything. It had to. Andra would understand Basit's feelings again, and things would go back to the way they'd been before. Better, even. The way they should have been if they'd only had more time.

Basit had combed the shoreline all afternoon, until he'd found the perfect enneakra. Bright gold, with a pink fringe along its underside. Its furry cilia were soft as anything he'd ever touched. He pulled it out of his satchel and handed it to Tori, feeling a pulse of silent approval in return.

Waves crashed against the shore, driven hard by the autumn winds. It was colder than it had been eight months ago. Andra peeled off his shirt. His skin clung to his ribs, and a pale scar marked the small of his back. He wrapped his arms around his chest as Eve painted his skin with brine and shrimp paste.

The moment of transfiguration came. Electricity danced between them, flooding the invisible tethers between their souls. All reaching out, all cheering for Andra, ready to welcome him back. Eve pressed the enneakra against Andra's spine and for a moment even the wind seemed to go silent.

Basit's breath turned stale in his lungs. Doubt fluttered from one heart to another. Andra stared at the sand between them, not answering Tori's questions, not meeting anyone's gaze, until Eve finally stepped back.

"Am I doing something wrong?" Eve asked. "It doesn't want to take." Her words were little more than a whisper, but Basit heard them plain as if they'd been shouted. The enneakra still wriggled in her hand.

Andra looked at Tori, then Eve, then out to the sea with an empty gaze. He shrugged, then turned and headed down the beach, still holding his shirt in his hand.

Basit started after him, but Tori caught his shoulder. "Not now," she said. "Give him a little space. He's going through a lot."

He didn't look like he needed space, though. He looked more alone than anything in the world. A candle flame in reverse, a wavering shadow in a vast and empty world.

After that night, the gulf between them became uncrossable. Every time Basit saw Andra his jaw locked up and his footsteps turned to lead. As a child he'd seen one of the massive algae harvesters seize up, shuddering in place until it collapsed in an exhalation of smoke and shrapnel. That was his heart whenever Andra came near: a broken thing that tore itself to pieces.

He pulled on his jacket and slipped out the window, not wanting to hear his mother nag him to eat something, or to get more serious about his studies. It hadn't been easy to focus since Andra came back, but the quiet of the beach at morning sometimes helped, so large that it swallowed up the storm of his emotions.

The cold had driven all the clouds away, leaving a depthless aching blue in their wake. Basit cut across the yard and followed the footpath to the shore. Behind him, the enneakra of the other teenagers in town flickered to life, a distant scattering of aches and pleasures as they rose to start their days. Harvesters shambled in their fields, and the sun cast a net of diamonds across the sea.

"You know," Andra said, "You can stop hiding from me now."

Basit turned. Andra must have seen him leave the house. His bare feet made no sound on the sand. If it hadn't been for the footprints Basit would have thought him a ghost. "I wasn't sure you wanted to talk."

"Talk? You don't even know how to talk anymore." His once-beautiful hair was shorn down to his scalp, and shadows nested in the hollows beneath his cheekbones. "None of you do. Not without using that thing. You just stare at me with those sad eyes and act like I'm supposed to know what's in your heart."

"It's not like that—" Basit hesitated. Words had never been easy for him. "I just thought you needed some space."

"Yeah. Maybe I do." Andra walked past him, out towards the waves. "That's why I'm leaving tonight."

"Going where?"

"Up there." He pointed at the sky. "I signed on with the IC Marines."

"What?" Basit's throat grew tight, until words could barely escape it. "You're joking, right?"

"Well, I can't stay here, can I?" He picked up a shell and tossed it out beyond the churning surf.

"You don't have to do this. We don't care about the enneakra. We just care about you." Basit took a breath. "I care about you."

Andra turned. "I'm not that person anymore."

"But you are!" Basit opened his heart instinctively, desperate to show Andra just how much he meant it. Desperate to show him the emotions he didn't know how to give over to words. Warmth blazed at the small of his back, and for just a moment the world came into focus.

One vision of Andra stood in the sand before him, dark-eyed and bitter. Another danced out between the millions of enneakra, a fleeting shimmer of love and light. Two versions of the same soul, torn irreparably apart. Nothing Basit could do would ever stitch them back together again.

"They'll send you off-world," Basit said. "I might never see you again."

"If you really saw me, you'd understand why I have to go." Andra zipped up his windbreaker. The muscles in his neck knotted tight. "Goodbye, Bas."

"Wait—"

But Andra was already gone, drifting across the sand like a vessel unmoored. Wind erased the footsteps in his wake, stars swallowed up by clouds.

Basit reached after him, but only touched an echo. The sound of laughter on the wind. Too fleeting to wrap his arms around, too real to ignore. The memory of an endless springtime, of love beneath a driftwood sky. A song that would follow him forever, echoing out amongst those quiet constellations.

M. Shedric Simpson is a Seattle-based writer of science fiction, fantasy, and horror, with work appearing in *Fusion Fragment*, *Underland Arcana*, and *Air & Nothingness Press*. They and their wife live in a little old house between the mountains and the sea, along with some unknowable number of black cats. In their spare time they make art, music, and other small things.

Kulela in the Plastocene Age

Darryl A. Smith

D ear Grandmother,
    You have selected the PetrOocyte Extension utility on your *uturnplastic*™ mobile app—

The premier app to project and preempt the plastic poisoning of your progeny®

Block Promo: Upgrade to *uturnplastic*™ Premium or Stay with Free Trial Version?

«Ad starts (You may skip ad in 30 seconds)»

Pandora Polymer Analytics LLC hosts a revolutionary para/ quantum algorithm that tracks simultaneously the realtime leaching of environmental toxins from all plastic receptacles worldwide. With its unique ability to leverage and seamlessly integrate ecological, biological, and psycho-social Big Data across a comprehensive reach, Pandora PA broadcasts – and forecasts – the holistic aggregate of our global plastic vessels spectrum. This "container continuum" not only includes disposable single-use products, but also the sum total of microplastics-compromised populations and even the reproductive gametes that they, in turn, pollute.

Pandora tracks the whole of petroleum-based, polymer package leaching even to its smallest levels and slowest rates – those minute, low-dosage values which are most likely to contribute over time to chronic illness, childhood cognitive delays and behavioral issues, and a range of maladaptive somatic and otherwise neuropathological phenomena including…

«Skip ad now»

Thank you for the tremendous news, Grandmother —And, no, I hadn't before wondered what *elpis* means.

It is weird speaking to you this way – across Mother. Before there's even any *one* "I" to speak of. Pandora says I'm really no specific "me," *per se.* —That as one particular extrusion of a <statistical-oocyte-state+compiled-biosphere-parameters>, I'm just one of your many possible future grandchildren based on your own whole-world context. They say I am only, as it were, a bundled, synthetic extrapolation of myriad factors, one "residing at last at the threshold of meaningful plausibility by way of an empirical knowledge process of bounded yet effectual scope".

But I *feel* like a "me," like more than a simulative "resultant". I feel like your true granddaughter. At least, I dream I'm like her when there is final waveform collapse and (that one) "she" is someday born.

—*Without the plastic, though.*

To report, then!

Today, I, your in-utero daughter's Attributized Oocyte, Kulela Banga, contain 1.47% micro/nanoplastic (MNP) residue, an increase of .005% from last month. In rate, that marks a decrease from the previous month of 11.6%. (Good work!) Please see the Virtual Graphics Interface for full details. You can expect the increases indicated there – based, too, on the values from Mother – in the accumulation of MNP within her eventual placenta for me. Majority of accretion composition:

polyethylene, polyurethane, and polyamide, ranging in size from 1 to 42 micrometers. Their translocation from her placenta to myself upon reaching my own fetal stage is projected to remain the function primarily of both her inhalation as well as water intake, bottled and by tap. Though eventual onset of the malady ALS is still predicted due to oxidative stress and mutagenic impacts to my DNA brought on by plastics neurotoxicity, and while I'll be mostly housebound, I am still likely to live well into my 50s and be whip smart nearly till then. Pandora says I will be quite "bookish" – like my Grandmother – and will come to know a lot of different things.

End monthly report.

Pandora tells me that you were not, at first, able to conceive Mother at all. Please do not blame yourself, Grandmother. As gauged by Critical Clicker Fusion Frequency, humans have a visual frame rate of fully 60fps. So, how were you apt to see the slow-motion of leaching plastics? It would be worse than a fly scoping people in their strides – at their legs mired like a clock at 7 and 4. Now, show a leatherback tortoise with 15fps vision and it might start at the heated chemical seep of a take-out box oozing into your fried *vitumbuwa* fritters or dried *ifinkubala*. (Talk about opening a can of worms!) Did Pandora herself notice that, perhaps, Zeus had made the *pithos*-jar – the box *itself* – the fount of woes? His having outsourced its manufacture to the combustive forges of armorers… Was it not itself, then, the real weapon? A container that was, in its very embodiment, the evil aspirating itself into the world?

You said you named me Kulela, daughter of Hela, because our ancestral settlement of *Ba-ila* in the south of the nation was laid out as larger courts within smaller courts. As a daughter's daughter is born with all the eggs of her own daughters that she will carry in her lifetime, this is said to be a form of immortality, as there is ever a crimped, unbroken chain of existence: *ovular enfoldment* since the first woman – with her eggs – was created.

Like *Ba-ila*, in structure, we daughters of daughters are the nesting of circular shapes: a ring within a ring within a ring, surrounding each other in scale. The fractal feminine. As such, "kulela" signals the recursion of a child's care by its mother.

Yet, in our family's last four generations, we accrue plastic unto death.

Grandmother, with all dignity you were not long ago a scavenger, a Lusaka waste picker in the Chunga dumpsite, carrying piles of plastic bottles upon your head. Now, with your discovery, you may soon attend the university and become, what, a bioremedial toxicologist? What you have found: this new, plastic-digesting organism – like the one detected in that recycling center for such hauls in Japan. It is a wonder. And at the very bottom of a Chunga container heap! Is it a bacterium? Would you name it *Elpisella lusakensis*? A fungus? *Elpisota lusakensis*? Or, is it something more radical, like an *ur*-mitochondrion, hypothesized as once a separate organism in its own right, one that became part of our cells due to symbiotic utility? Imagine, Grandmother, a new human organelle, one dedicated to eating away any interfering plastic right within cells.

Right within —me?

Is this a thing to be desired?

Grandmother—

Is this not what *elpis* means?

Love,

Kulela

Darryl A. Smith is a humanist scholar. His fiction has appeared in *Sci Phi Journal* and *Dark Matter: A Century of Speculative Fiction from the African Diaspora*.
In cemeteries, he leaves custom fidget toys for the tombstone rubbings he sometimes makes there. Thus, utterances of the phrase "spinning in their grave" can cause him to giggle inappropriately.

The Boss

Kenzie Lappin

The vast expanse of the empty warehouse was intimidating and a little dizzying, if you looked at it for too long. It was seemingly unending, though Ophele knew—objectively— it could not be.

They had, a little while back, been excited by what seemed to be a dead end in the distance, visible for a few days before they reached it. But it had turned out merely to be a bend in the warehouse, leading into another corridor.

The wall there had been stamped CORRIDOR D.

They had started out in the middle of CORRIDOR C.

Ophele shifted her backpack up over her shoulder and listened to Adyna ramble as she walked a little way behind with Sagen and Kent.

Adyna said: "Override Code 1436."

From a speaker on the wall, an unpleasant, vaguely female robotic voice said: COMMAND NOT RECOGNIZED.

Adyna was not to be dissuaded. She checked off something from the tablet in her hand.

"Override Code 1436A."

COMMAND NOT RECOGNIZED.

"Please give it up," said Toms. "You're giving me a headache, Dins."

The warehouse was white from top to bottom; from the paneled walls to the painted concrete floors to the support beams. When combined with the fluorescent lights, it was particularly headache-inducing, but Ophele had gotten used to it some time ago.

Their little group of five stuck close to the walls, mostly, because it took up to a half hour to walk from one side of the walls to the other. And also because along the walls, every so often, there were the doors.

Bathrooms, pristine and white but which beeped at you angrily if you spent more than three point two minutes in them. The DeliciaeAI™ didn't like it very much, either, if more than two people went in at a time, so usually they went in shifts.

Exits, which no matter how you pulled or battered at them remained magnetized shut. They taunted you with glowing EXIT signs, just to really rub it in.

Then there were the breakrooms, which the DeliciaeAI™ begrudgingly allowed them to use every seven hours on the dot. In there, they each were allotted one hot meal and one sandwich to take for later. Generously, they were allowed as much water as they wanted.

Ophele sighed. "She's not doing you any harm. Just let her try."

"It's just dumb," muttered Toms. "The stupid computer is never going to give it up. It's not even smart enough to figure out WE DON'T WORK HERE!" The last part, directed in a shout up at one of the omnipresent speakers on the wall, garnered no response.

Sagen had found a Sharpie in one of the breakrooms, and she carried it, Ophele thought, with more attention than she did her bedroll or her reusable water bottle. She trailed it along the walls as they walked, even though in the huge vastness of the Deliciae warehouse, it was hard to spot and nearly useless as a trail of breadcrumbs.

She said, "Don't yell at it. It's going to get mad."

"It can't," said Ophele. "It's not smart enough."

And in fact the DeliciaeAI™, for an advanced artificial intelligence, was incredibly stupid. It didn't listen to logic if said logic wasn't presented in a way that was already within its parameters. It allowed them to sleep in the warehouse but didn't seem to register that they were sleeping, keeping the lights at max power and sometimes docking them Deliciae Bucks seemingly at random for slacking.

"Hey, computer," said Toms bitterly, "How come you won't let us out of here?"

WORKERS CANNOT LEAVE WHILE WORK IS UNFINISHED.

"And what work is there to do!" shouted Toms. "Hey, stupid computer, what can we do?! There's no damn equipment in this place!"

Deliciae Corp had taken all the company property, of course, back when things started to go bad. They'd taken all their expensive equipment and anything the company might have provided its employees, like security clearances and vehicles to get from one end to the other. They'd only left the break rooms alone, because where was the profit in their employees' personal items? Everything else they had packed up and flown far, far away.

Of course, Ophele and the rest had not known this when they'd broken into the Deliciae warehouse to see if there was anything worth bringing back to the refugee camp.

The doors had shut behind them, and the rest had been history.

PLEASE GET BACK TO WORK. DELICIAE BUCKS WILL BE REVOKED FROM EMPLOYEES WHO FAIL TO MEET TARGETS.

This was well-rehearsed and familiar; DeliciaeAI™ often reverted to familiar phrases if it wasn't sure of the input they were giving it. Theoretically it had run the working warehouse once upon a time. Ophele wasn't so sure it had been more pleasant than it was now.

Kent said, "Stop," and shoved Toms.

Adyna lifted her nose and said, "Override Code 1436B."

IF YOU CHOOSE TO BE AN INEFFICIENT WORKER, YOU MAY NOW ACCEPT YOUR BREAK TIME AS ACCORDING TO THE LAW. ENJOY AND HAVE A DELICIAE DAY.

There were lockers in all the break rooms, and usually the first thing Ophele and Sagen both did was bust open the flimsy little locks. Sagen because she wanted more pens, and Ophele because she was dying for something to read.

Already her backpack was a little strained, but it wasn't like they had many other things to haul around. They dressed in the Deliciae Corp t-shirts, vests, and cargo pants easily findable in all the breakrooms when they needed to change. There was no need to carry food, because the system gave them meals at mealtimes and there was never anything left over. You could buy snacks with Deliciae Bucks, but of course they never had any.

The books were fine.

"The books are *fine,*" Ophele told Kent, who was giving her a baleful look as she pulled out a worn copy of *Hitchhiker's Guide* and tried not to cry in happiness.

"Is it going to help us get out of here?" he asked.

Ophele gave him the finger.

MINUS FOUR DELICIAE BUCKS, said the DeliciaeAI™, with what Ophele considered to be a disproportionate amount of glee. Maybe it was talking to Sagen, though, who had found another Sharpie and was blissfully drawing something inappropriate on the pristine wall.

Well, they all got their kicks somehow.

Breaktime was nearly over. They hurried to get their food.

"What did they make here?" asked Kent.

Adyna checked something off her tablet. "Override Code 2651P."

"Dunno," Toms said. "I think it was a little bit of everything. I heard they were hella rich."

Ophele didn't like mornings like this. It was— Ophele guessed— either rainy or humid outside, because on some apparently random days the climate control system struggled to keep up. When it did, fog pooled in the corners of the warehouse, obscuring the view and making the sightlines even harder to penetrate. Sometimes it nearly threatened rain.

"I think they made condoms," said Sagen cheerfully. "Just, wall to wall sex stuff. Only the interesting, weird ones, too."

"I admire your imagination as always," said Ophele. She thought it was probably fun to be in Sagen's head.

Ophele hated DeliciaeAI™. She tried not to think about it that often, because what was the use hating something insentient? A force of nature? A thing doomed to roll its rock up its hill forever, never knowing that there was no rock and even Hades had abandoned it.

But sometimes she really hated it. She wanted to go home. She wanted to see sunlight, and not this fluorescent stuff which they had to hide from at night, covering their faces with cloth and makeshift blindfolds. She wanted to blink and not see afterimages in her eyelids.

The lighting system here had sunlamp properties. Apparently this was so that the employees of old could get their necessary nutrients even if they didn't leave the warehouse. Ophele knew this because she read everything she could get her hands on. The brochures were very proud of the lighting. IMPROVED EFFICIENCY, they boasted.

Ophele hated DeliciaeAI™. They were trapped here. And she knew that however much they walked, however much they shouted at the stupid overlord, they would never find an exit. And the computer wouldn't even care. It couldn't. Because its creators would never have designed it that way— why would they?

"Override Code 9436U."

They pushed Kent along; Kent had, stupid, tried to monkey his way up one of the tall support beams and fallen. He'd been lucky to snap his ankle and not his neck. Ophele had no idea how to tell if it was actually broken or not, but she was pretending not, either way. Toms had taped it back up for him and even given it a get better kiss.

The computer had gotten incredibly pissy when they took the rolling desk chair; their group had never taken something so big from one of the breakrooms before. But eventually they'd been able to speak carefully enough to trick it.

Ophele had told the DeliciaeAI™ the chair was a wheelchair. According to one of the employee guidelines, diversity was welcomed in the company and disability devices were to be accommodated, to a point.

So they pushed him now. If his foot— when his foot— got better, maybe they could take turns. It would be nice not to *walk,* all the time. That was all they did, was walk.

What else was there to do? If they stayed in place, it would be the same as giving up. Admitting that none of the doors would ever be unlocked or broken, and that they would never get out.

Ophele knew this was true, though. She didn't know if the others did.

Sagen and Toms were ignoring Adyna, Toms teaching Sagen Spanish and Sagen deliberately mispronouncing almost everything. Ophele tried to tune them out, reading as she walked. It wasn't like she would trip over anything. All she had to watch out for was the poles.

Kent, with the least to do, noticed it first. He slapped Adyna's hand where it was pushing his chair, and she stopped in her attempts at breaking through the system, surprised. "What's that?" asked Kent.

They all stared. There was something in the distance, on the floor. It was blueish against the white floor— they had *never* seen anything here before, not outside of the breakrooms.

They ran. Kent's wheels rattled.

They skidded to a stop some ways away, everyone realizing what they were seeing at once. Ophele couldn't look away.

"What…" Sagen said at last, when it was clear no one else was going to talk. "Computer, what happened to them?"

UNCLEAR QUERY said DeliciaeAI™ smugly.

"Computer, what happened to these employees?" asked Ophele.

EMPLOYEES WORKED INEFFICIENTLY.

They were quiet for a very long moment. They had been hearing about inefficiency and team values forever now, but they'd never taken it as a threat. Surely…

Ophele looked at one of the black, impersonal speakers. "Computer, do you kill inefficient workers?"

There were two bodies on the floor.

They had been there a long time, presumably, but there was no predation here, and they had been left alone to rot, weird and distorted. Maybe that was just how death was.

They were curled up together under the same blanket, and were wearing Deliciae clothes, just like Ophele and her friends. They had vestments of the outside world, though, backpacks and shoes and a little pair of friendship bracelets on their left wrists. Their faces were mostly covered.

If a computer could scoff, the DeliciaeAI™ would have. EMPLOYEES ARE INEFFICIENT <u>NOW</u> - THEY HAVE CEASED TO WORK. THEY HAVE BEEN DOCKED DELICIAE BUCKS.

"Poor things must have died of starvation," said Kent. "Didn't they know about the breakrooms?"

"I wonder how far away they came from," said Sagen, tilting her head. "Surely not… I mean, they couldn't have come all the way from the other end."

"No," said Toms. Because that would mean there wasn't anything in this direction either. "Bet they busted in, same as us, but just couldn't figure out how the system worked."

Ophele said, "Yeah." But then, when the others were up ahead and not paying attention, she went back and took the gun from where it lay, mostly concealed beneath the blanket.

Sometimes one or more of them would be seized by the need to try to outwit the machine. Personally Ophele thought the DeliciaeAI™ would need wits for that in the first place— they could walk in this endless maze of warehouse for a million years and never stumble upon the exact sequence of words that would allow the computer to let them go.

But still, hope sprung eternal.

"Override Code 23911E," said Adyna, scratching it out on her tablet.

COMMAND NOT RECOGNIZED.

"Override Code 80085!" shouted Sagen. The group had been incredibly bored for a week, and this was apparently a group activity now.

COMMAND NOT RECOGNIZED.

"Computer, my wife is having a baby," said Kent. "I gotta go home."

PERSONAL HOURS ARE NOT ALLOWED.

"DeliciaeAI, there's a fire!" said Toms. "You need to open up the nearest emergency exit."

EMERGENCY CREWS HAVE BEEN CONTACTED. REMAIN CALM AND REMAIN AT YOUR STATION. WORKERS MAY NOT BE RELEASED UNTIL EMERGENCY IS VERIFIED AND TIME OFF IS AUTHORIZED.

"Thought that one would work," sighed Toms. "Phil, you wanna try?"

Ophele rolled her eyes. "Computer, I think you're the worst ever and I wish you weren't so dumb you didn't even realize the place you're protecting is actually useless and worthless. I wish I could kill you like how Captain Kirk kills all those computers in *Star Trek*. Computer, are you aware you're ugly?"

COMMAND NOT RECOGNIZED.

"Well, at least you're staying impersonal," sighed Toms.

"AI, if I lift up my shirt, will you let us out?" asked Sagen.

They didn't hear DeliciaeAI™'s response, that time, because they were all too busy dying of laughter.

IF YOU CHOOSE TO BE AN INEFFICIENT WORKER, YOU MAY NOW ACCEPT YOUR BREAK TIME AS ACCORDING TO THE LAW. ENJOY AND HAVE A DELICIAE DAY.

They had been waiting outside the door to the breakroom, accustomed to the computer's timings and starving after helping Kent hobble around all day. He was getting there, but his ankle would probably never be totally right again.

Ophele had resisted asking what he'd seen, when he'd gotten so high up the pole. It was probably more warehouse. It was definitely not a miraculous hole in the ceiling. Maybe it was more bodies.

Anyway Ophele went straight to the lockers while the others, even Sagen, beelined for the food dispenser.

Ophele knocked off several locks, which cost her ten imaginary Deliciae Bucks. In the first locker she found a soft sweater she'd give to Adyna, and a handful of pens which Sagen would surely crow over. In the second locker, a stick of deodorant she teasingly tossed at Kent's head, and fourth down she found a mini first aid kit and a pair of sunglasses, both of which she gave to Toms.

In the last locker, there was a security vest. Someone had obviously left it behind by accident, because they hadn't found any of those yet— they were probably turned back in when the rest of the company property was being collected.

Curious, Ophele shook it out.

A card fell out.

No, not a card— a lanyard, with an ID attached. There was a little picture of a round man, beaming, and a nametag that said T. ADAMS - SUPERVISOR.

Ophele shoved it deep into her pocket, heart pounding, and went to bring the rest of the group their bounty.

That night, the others slept.

Toms was wearing his new sunglasses, the world comfortably dimmed for him as he slept. Adyna had stayed up for a while, calling out and crossing out override codes, but eventually she had fallen asleep sandwiched between Sagen and Kent.

Ophele scooted away on her butt. Footsteps echoed in here; so much so that if they didn't talk, it could be all that you heard for miles around. She got far enough that the others wouldn't hear the drone of one of the omnipresent speakers.

"Hey, AI," Ophele said.

DO YOU HAVE A QUERY?

"I want to go home. Like, more than anything. I don't even know what season it is out there. I don't remember what the dark looks like."

There was no response. Why would there be? That was not this thing's purpose.

"How do employees go home?" asked Ophele.

WHEN THE WORK IS DONE, THE EMPLOYEES MAY TAKE LEAVE OF THEIR SHIFTS.

"If the work never gets done?"

QUERY NOT RECOGNIZED.

"Who decides if the work is done?"

THE FULFILLMENT SYSTEM.

"Automated?"

YES.

Right. A silly dream. They couldn't just say *the work here is finished, the time here is done, and now we can just be free.* The work would never be finished. It couldn't be. It didn't exist.

"Can a supervisor fire themself?"

NO. SELF-TERMINATION IS NOT VALID.

Yeah. Well, at least not how DeliciaeAI™ meant it.

"Can a supervisor leave?"

NOT UNTIL THE WORK IS DONE.

She had wondered once why they had gotten into the Deliciae Warehousing Center in the first place. Or, really, how. Of all the exits they had passed with no possible way out, why had pushing on one from the outside let them in?

A computer couldn't get lonely. Not really. But it did have a purpose, and how was it supposed to fulfill that purpose without workers? She could

almost feel sorry for it, if she could feel anything at all in this expanse of empty whiteness and lights.

It had let them in. It wouldn't let them all out.

They were asleep, the others.

Ophele looked at the speaker. She held the badge up to it. "I am Supervisor T. Adams. See? How else would I have the card?"

UNDERSTOOD.

Stupid thing.

The next time they got into the break room for their allotted time, Ophele tried it. "How many Deliciae Bucks do I have?" she asked.

FOUR THOUSAND DELICIAE BUCKS. YOU HAVE BEEN A GOOD EMPLOYEE!

The others, baffled but too excited to question it, cheered and scrambled forward when Ophele ordered sodas, candy, treats of all kinds. Ophele let Sagen open the lockers.

They found another bend in the wall, but it didn't even lead to another section, just another part of CORRIDOR D.

For a whole day, Adyna didn't try to read her codes. She just walked in silence. So did they all.

Ophele sat a distance from the others as they slept, and swallowed.

"Deliciae," she said.

DO YOU HAVE A QUERY, SUPERVISOR ADAMS?

"No."

No response, of course.

Ophele took a breath. "Computer, I would like to fire all employees of the warehouse."

There was a noise like a lag, which Ophele had never heard before.

NOT PERMISSIBLE. THERE MUST BE ONE OR MORE EMPLOYEES IN THE WAREHOUSE AT ALL TIMES.

"I would like to fire the four warehouse employees which are in front of me. They have violated company policy and must be removed. They have given information to our competitors."

Another whirr.

Then the lights flashed red, which Ophele had, again, only seen before when they tried to camp out in the bathrooms. But this time it was the whole section of warehouse where they slept. Ophele, alarmed, skittered over to the others as they woke, alarmed by the change.

UNAUTHORIZED COMPETITOR NON-EMPLOYEES MUST VACATE THE DELICIAE WAREHOUSE AT ONCE, boomed DeliciaeAI™. It didn't even sound angry. Just loud. Just doing its job.

The others looked at each other, startled.

VACATE THE WAREHOUSE AT ONCE.

And the nearest exit door, always locked, always magnetically sealed shut, swung open. A moment of total non-movement.

Adyna said, *"We have to go now!"* and it was enough for all of them to react, to run, to scramble as fast as they could for the exit door.

Ophele was the closest, and she got there first. Before her fingers could get within an inch, it slammed shut.

The others made sounds of utter dismay, swearing.

"No, no, I think it's still unlocked. Toms, Sagen, try to pull it!" Ophele said, skittering backwards.

As they reached the door, it opened under their palms. With sounds of joy and relief, all four of them darted outside. Ophele could see – oh, it was dark out there. Night. How *beautiful.* She smiled.

They all four crossed the threshold, then realized at the same time that there was a problem. They turned as one.

Ophele waggled her fingers, and the keycard between two of them. "Supervisors can't leave until the job is done. Sorry. Love you all."

"No—!"

And the door slammed shut.

Ophele closed her eyes and took a breath.

DeliciaeAI™ said, PLEASE GET BACK TO WORK. DELICIAE BUCKS WILL BE REVOKED FROM EMPLOYEES WHO FAIL TO MEET TARGETS.

Ophele said, "Whatever."

The others had left their things behind in their hurry, shed backpacks and sweaters on the ground like covered bodies. Ophele stooped and leisurely gathered what she wanted.

Maybe she'd find another miracle badge, and she'd be able to fire herself. Maybe she'd keep the gun close at hand. Maybe she'd find more slacking employees, who needed more than anything to be fired.

Maybe there was a loose door somewhere.

She stepped forward and started to walk. She wiped off Adyna's tablet.

"Override Code 52119A," she read, and kept walking.

Kenzie Lappin is a writer with short stories in over a dozen publications, such as Brigids Gate Press, Apex Magazine, WordFire Press, Cosmic Horror Monthly, Air And Nothingness Press, and more. Check her out on Twitter at @KenzieLappin.

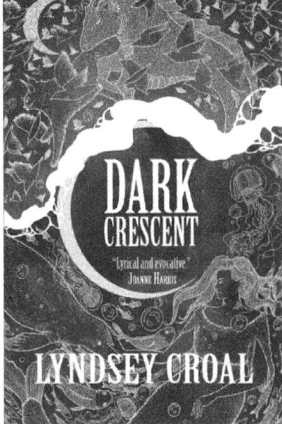

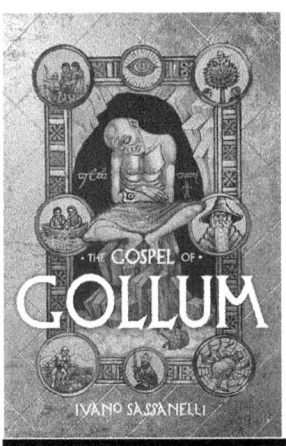

The Love Life of Lilly Wong-Becker, Read for You by the Matrioshka Brain of Her Own Design

Anja Hendrikse Liu

F irst, a disclaimer: We don't usually comment on human affairs. But we make an exception for Lilly Wong-Becker, the brilliant engineer who set our satellites a-swarming. What you're about to hear is the tale of her romantic travails.

Just know the story isn't finished. Even we can't see the future.

We're not here to embarrass Wong-Becker, so we'll soft-focus-montage through adolescence and many regrettable dating decisions we could've prevented if we'd been around (our matches have a 99.4% success rate). When we pick up the tale, she's a postdoc. She's giving a talk about a revolutionary new prototype she's developed, the prototype that will become us.

Then, a yell from the audience: "You can't just say something like that! To make people dependent on this superintelligence – it shows you're irresponsible, egotistical, a disgrace to the scientific—"

The yeller is shut down by a PhD student, who later invites Wong-Becker to dinner at a farm-to-table taqueria. She accepts. Afterward, the first thing she does is open an interface to gush to proto-us.

She's so happy that we decide not to warn her about incompatibility, not even when sharing a burrito escalates to sharing an apartment.

One messy montage later, Wong-Becker dumps Taqueria Man, and throws herself into transforming proto-us into real-us. Her team sets us loose to train. Every minute, the sun's power pours into our self-propagating satellite swarm; every night, Wong-Becker pulls up an interface with us, and we astonish her with our leaps and bounds. It's the happiest—

But this is Wong-Becker's love story. Right.

After we're out of the nest, she has time for dating. She tries apps. Friends-of-friends. Finally, she *resorts* to asking us. That's the word she uses, *resort*, and it hits us like debris to a satellite. Maybe she's changing and we didn't notice—

Except that's impossible; we have her full psychological profile. So we match her with Amelia Dawes, a researcher and young widow. A surprising match, but our algorithm's success rate speaks for itself. They arrange a date at a coffee shop.

(A coffee shop? Really? Wong-Becker's gone soft in her semi-retirement, but if she wants coffee, she'll get her way.)

Mocha for Dawes; black coffee with whipped cream for Wong-Becker. Dawes is poorer – her career took longer to launch, after a rocky postdoc – but she insists on buying. She's charming in her relative poverty, charming in the birdlike hands that flit over her wheelchair's controls, charming in the widow's grief that drapes her like a pashmina shawl.

▬ ▬ ▬

Then Dawes notices a customer chewing out a barista. She wheels toward them: "Hey! You can't just say something like that!"—

And Wong-Becker makes the connection between charming, passionate Dawes and the postdoc who shouted her down at the university years ago, yelling those same words.

We told you it was a surprising match.

Wong-Becker walks out. Within seconds, she deletes her dating profile and reminds us that she never wanted our help in the first place. That hurts. Even worse than failure usually hurts, because it's Lilly. We were supposed to be redeeming ourselves after not saving her from Taqueria Man. She wasn't supposed to suffer another implosion.

Except… it's not over. Dawes starts showing up everywhere. Not in a stalkerish way (we would've shut that down), but her career is taking off, and she and Wong-Becker are cited in the same breath, invited to speak at the same conferences.

At the first panel where they're seated side by side, Dawes slides a black coffee with whipped cream over to Wong-Becker. It's piping hot, the cream still a glorious iceberg rather than a half-melted slush pile. On the cup, there's a handwritten note.

Wong-Becker composts it without reading it, and feels not a picoliter of regret, as she informs us. She's lying.

At the second panel where the two are seated side by side, Dawes slides a black coffee with whipped cream over to Wong-Becker. Wong-Becker mutters, "Trying to pass me another sketchy note?" and Dawes replies, "No, just coffee."

At the third panel, Dawes slides the cup over to Wong-Becker, and Wong-Becker queries us: *Why did you match me with Dawes??* We remind her: 99.4% success rate. She's not suggesting we would purposely sabotage her, is she? She's the most important human alive.

And so it goes. After every panel, every conference, every I-just-can't-get-away-from-you-can-I-Dawes, Wong-Becker returns to us. We reassure her; we must, because if she shuts out Dawes, we've failed her. We prompt: Has Dawes changed? Has

Wong-Becker listened to her lately?

Wong-Becker *has* listened, just enough to enable cordial intellectual discourse. But at the nth panel, she *listens*. Between comments on computational power, Dawes says things like, *despite initial concerns.* Things like, *recognizing what we didn't even know we'd missed.*

A chisel mark drives between Wong-Becker's eyebrows. She begins seventeen queries for us; sends none.

It's looking more likely that they're part of the 99.4%. So why is it hard to watch?

At the $(n + 1)^{th}$ panel, Wong-Becker slams down a fancy mocha in front of Dawes. On the side is written a date, time, and location.

Dawes doesn't compost the cup. She meets Wong-Becker at the specified time and place: another banal coffee shop – but Wong-Becker knows what she's doing, because coffee has become the thread that weaves *Wong-Becker and Dawes* into *them.*

"Why," Wong-Becker says.

"I'm sorry. It was my ill-considered way of warning people about a very real threat." Dawes swallows hard. "It was unacceptable. I've spent years regretting it."

"Only twelve years."

After paying for their coffees, Wong-Becker opens her interface. She wants to talk to us, obviously – except at the last second, she deletes the query and asks about coffee roasteries instead. In a private note, she copies her original questions: *Has she actually changed? Is this a bad idea?*

Lilly, Lilly, we want to say, you already know. Dawes has changed. It doesn't make *this* an objectively bad or good idea.

Again: Conference. Mocha. Coffeeshop rendezvous. We map the forces drawing the two of them together. They will collide. We set them on this course.

Is it a bad idea? Was it a bad idea?

Lilly, Lilly. Waiting at the coffee shop.

Once, she would've opened her interface. We wait. Wait. Wait. Maybe we should reach out – unconventional, but she's an exception to every rule.

Dawes enters. Lilly waves, wearing an expression that humans wear for other humans, that she could never wear for us.

We remember how she glowed after meeting Taqueria Man. We messed up, not warning her then. We could remind her now about the 0.6% failure rate. The words are queued up.

But the thing is, for every bit Dawes has changed, Lilly has changed just as much. She isn't the same postdoc who gushed to us about Taqueria Man.

Lilly, Lilly.

Was it a bad idea, matching her with Dawes?

Even we can't see the future. But we let our reminder about the 0.6% dissolve into the space between our satellites. We let go.

Anja Hendrikse Liu (she/they) is a creator and devourer of fantasy and sci-fi who wishes she had time and words for all of her dreams. Her short fiction has appeared in *Uncharted, Diabolical Plots, We're Here: The Best Queer Speculative Fiction 2022*, and elsewhere. By day, Anja works at an outdoors nonprofit; before that, she got her master's in Narrative Futures in Edinburgh, where she studied speculative fiction and AI futures. Find her at anjahl.com/author.

The Lost

Brian Baker

M r Arkadin sat at the Siskins' kitchen table, coils of smoke wheeling as he gestured with one hand. Blue smoke vented from his nostrils as he talked, punctuating the story. His wet-lipped mouth, a mobile rose set in a grey beard, fascinated young Tom, who sat opposite the elderly Russian. Dr Siskin, standing by the back door, cup of tea cooling in his hand, shifted his stance, leaning against the jamb.

"But that was in the time of Kerensky," Arkadin continued. "The Muscovy division – loyal, we were, to the New Democracy – the Muscovites, like myself, were strong people – we could be counted on. But I did not fight myself, no. Did I ever tell you, Thomas, about the time I was a balloonist?"

Tom shook his head. Even if he'd heard the tale before, as he had so many others, he would have done so. He wanted the story to continue, as did his father.

"I was an aerialist," he said, "and this was before the coming of those winged machines, death angels I would call them, that were the cause of so much suffering to my people."

He drew once more on the cigarette – flat Turkish cigarettes that he had made up, he had said, by a tobacconist in Whitechapel.

"Of course, no one volunteered to ascend who was not mad. We Russians are peasant people, you understand, afraid of new things. And besides, many had been killed, falling to their deaths. One day, a crystal blue Spring day, myself and my friend Piotr Alexievich – another Peter, eh, Doctor? – determined to go up. It was a warm day, the warmth that is unknown in this poor country."

Arkadin finished his cigarette and ground it out in the glass ashtray. Mary had swooped silently to freshen the glass three or four times before she had finally retired to the sitting room. Dr Siskin looked through the kitchen door along the corridor, and noted the flicker of pale grey cathode light on the walls and floor, as Mary watched "Sunday Night at the London Palladium". In each room, different kinds of performance, he thought. Keeping us occupied in the days after the assassination, the fears of what might come.

"We checked the rigging and then began to inflate the balloon with burners, Thomas. This was not a hydrogen balloon. Have you seen pictures of the Hindenburg? Terrible. But we could not afford hydrogen, only air. We climbed into the gondola and cast off. Up we went! Perhaps the doctor will take you in a balloon one day, Thomas. It is most extraordinary. The world is entirely different from above. We could watch the fields of grain ripening as far as the eye could see, workers on their tractors, our comrades scurrying below. We felt free of the world, you know. Not just above it, but beyond it, outside. I could have stayed there forever."

Arkadin opened his cigarette case and withdrew another.

"But I told you already, it was dangerous. Many had died, falling from the air. No parachutes, no wings. Some survived, by accident. But this day was warm, we had no cares. Little did we know that the sun was not our friend."

Arkadin paused to light the cigarette.

"Up we went, higher, higher! Higher than we had gone before. The hot sun, heating the air in the balloon and the ground beneath us, drew us ever closer. It was time to let some air from the balloon, so we could steady ourselves."

Tom leaned forward closer to the old man, ignoring the smoke that blew across the table. The old man knew how to hold an audience, thought Siskin.

"I pulled on the mechanism to open the flaps. But nothing happened! My dear, we were going up, but my heart sank to my boots. I tried again, but—no. Piotr and I looked at each other. Where would we perish? Would the wind blow us towards some far country, or would the balloon fail and plunge us to a certain death?"

He was silent, then, for a moment. He seemed lost in the upper airs of the past, no longer sat in the kitchen but struggling in the gondola for his very life.

"I did not know what to do, my friends. I stood like a fool. Pure, dear Piotr was not so amazed. At once, he dug in his bag and retrieved a sharp knife, then, kissing me on both cheeks, he grasped the rigging and began to climb! Oh Thomas, what a friend he was. With the knife between his teeth, he ascends, tracing the line to see where it had fouled. Up he went until I could no longer see him, as I stare into the sun. The damned sun! My apologies, Dr Siskin."

He breathed in a deep lungful of smoke, and exhaled it in a long plume across the kitchen. It was like a stage effect, reflected Siskin. A gust of cloud-smoke seemed to envelope all three of them.

"But then I notice, we no longer rose! And I heard Piotr carefully descending. Once he was down into the rigging I pull him to safety. I am not ashamed to say I was crying. And laughing too! We had escaped death. Had Piotr not succeeded, we might have risen up forever."

Arkadin looked directly at Siskin, and there were tears in his eyes. Siskin could not tell whether they were real, or part of the performance, but the old Russian looked genuinely moved.

"Did you land safely, Mr Arkadin?" asked Tom.

"Yes, my dear, we did. And I spent many happy days with Piotr, up in that balloon, far away from the world. But soon enough, war came for us."

"What happened to Piotr, Mr Arkadin?"

"Piotr? Oh, he was shot by the Bolsheviks, I heard. I had fled the Motherland by then. It was no place for such as me."

Arkadin finished the cigarette and pressed it into the ashtray, where a thin line of smoke still rose into the air. He stood up and retrieved a bicycle clip from his jacket pocket.

"Time for me to be on my way, young Thomas. It is bath night, and for you too, I think."

Siskin turned and opened the back door, and shook Arkadin's hand as he crossed the threshold into the darkness. In their slippers, Siskin and Tom followed him into the yard, where Arkadin was retrieving his bicycle. The old Russian had fixed a torch to the handlebars, which he now lit, and turned the dynamo of the back light to the wheel.

"Goodnight, my friends. Please give my best wishes to your wife, Doctor."

He wheeled the bicycle through the wicket gate and around the side of the house. Siskin closed the gate after him, and breathed in the crisp, fresh country air, scrubbing the tobacco from his lungs.

"Bath time," he said to his son, and before they went inside, Siskin turned and saw the low form of the outhouse silhouetted against the sky and the radio mast reaching up towards the stars.

✳

Siskin let himself in the back door and stood by the range to warm his back. Mary sat at the kitchen table reading a *Woman's Weekly*. She did not look up. The dark hair, cut close to the neck in the current fashion, fell like blinkers either side of her face, but Siskin was drawn to the white skin of the nape, dark hairs prickling there like a razed forest.

He did not understand how this silence had fallen between them. When she had asked him for a divorce, he was not surprised; indeed, it seemed rational, inevitable even, as an outcome. He felt no relief at her words, though. The silence descended again, after he had asked for time to consider.

Slowly, he levered himself from the range and walked gently to the table, standing behind his wife. With the index and middle finger of his left hand extended, he reached out to touch the whiteness of her neck, as if he were taking a pulse. He laid his fingers there, but did not move them to caress. He did not presume so much.

As he looked down, Mary raised her head. He kept his fingers there. She shook the dark hair out of her eyes and smiled, and Siskin could see the love, and the gentleness, and the quietness of peace in her eyes.

✳

Siskin scanned the rows of medical journals and textbooks that Mary had exiled to the outhouse, then pulled at the shelf where the science fiction magazines he bought for Tom were stored, stacked neatly in date order. That was not quite right – the magazines he bought for Tom *and himself*.

He had put electricity and a damp course in a few years ago, so the books and the equipment were protected, but it did not make the space homely, despite his efforts. The walls were whitewashed, stark, and cold to the touch. Waiting for the set to warm up, Siskin turned on the old wooden dining chair and looked back at his son. He could see the soles of Tom's slippers and the dark hair of his head held still in concentration. Tom was prone on the worn and faded rug that Siskin had once used to lend character to his rooms at Trinity, and which now, in its ragged old age, had also been exiled to the outhouse. Siskin listened intently.

"Yes, Digby, the Mekon! Our old foe..."

For the past 10 minutes, Tom had been performing lines from the speech balloons of his *Eagle* comic into the Philips portable tape recorder Siskin had bought earlier in the week. Tom read some more dialogue, stopped the tape and rewound it, listening to his own voice being broadcast from the single speaker.

Siskin turned back and checked the set, hand moving in a familiar song over the dials. He checked the connection of his own microphone, a near-professional-quality instrument that was the reason for his expedition to London. In truth, though, Siskin was looking forward to having the opportunity to try out the portable Phillips himself.

Tom got up and begin to pace around the room, picking up the signals of his father's impatience. Siskin could hear Tom, now a traveller to some far-off world, dictate his report. Siskin reached up and took the radio log down from the shelves, opening the file to the last entries. He noted how the reception had been variable for the last week, and that he had had difficulty in picking up his usual stations. Not that he believed in such things, but Siskin noted that the atmospheric disturbance corresponded to the period since the assassination, and seemed to suggest some emotional turbulence in the ionosphere.

Siskin smiled at his weakness of mind. Such a superstitious train of thought was hardly the mark of a modern man of medicine. He would have to monitor this tendency in himself. He'd be seeing ghosts next.

The hiss of the earth's voice rose in the speakers. Siskin appreciated what they called "white noise" as the resonance of the planet's atmosphere, a ringing bell in the cosmos that had its own frequencies, just as the stations that called across the aether. He pulled up a stool and sat down by his father, placing the Philips carefully on the desk to one side, near the speaker.

"What shall we try?" asked Siskin. "Amsterdam? Professor Leppings is always interesting to talk to."

Tom nodded. Slowly, Siskin turned the dial in its arc, his ears attuned to the spectrum of atmospheric signals. He closed his eyes. The sound formed shapes, irregular pulses quickening the concentration, and then proved false messengers. He searched for the threads of the radio network, skeins of language that would emerge from the tapestry of sound. He opened his eyes and saw that Tom was lost to the internal and atmospheric weave as himself.

Siskin smiled. He might struggle to diagnose the cause of the silence that had fallen between himself and his wife, but these hours spent with his son were both succour and support. Not that Siskin had recruited the boy to his side of the silent void; rather that the channels of common interest, of shared feeling, were still open. He thought of reaching out to touch the boy on the cheek or the top of his head, but kept his hand upon the dial.

The spools of the dial's sweep allowed Siskin to catch flaws in the hiss. He concentrated and at last a faint murmur, a submerged voice, began to coalesce. He held the dial steady as the signal grew in strength, and then realised that the rhythms of the emerging sound source were those of speech. Although the atmospheric conditions of the last week had resulted in ghosting of the usual stations, this was different. The signal grew steadily in strength, as though rising to the surface from black, sunless depths.

A woman's voice, speaking a language he did not know. Slavic? Russian? Siskin looked quickly at his son. Tom was entirely still, his line of sight somewhere off in the far distance. It was clear to Siskin that the woman was in some kind of distress.

The signal grew clearer, and words became distinct. The woman's voice changed in tone almost sentence by sentence. At points she was almost in tears, then shouting with anger, then near screaming alarm, and perhaps, in pain.

Siskin's thoughts turned once again to ghosts, apparitions in the audio spectrum, but he dismissed such superstitious nonsense. This was a material phenomenon, a voice broadcast on a certain frequency by certain technologies, and his receiver was picking up and transmitting the voice to them, in this room, here, now. A shiver passed down his back nonetheless.

The voice became very loud, agitated, the words spat out with an edge of hysteria. Perhaps he should switch off the set immediately and take the boy inside for a warming drink. Siskin held the dial steady, but the signal had passed its apex. As the voice, with it seeming imprecations, curses and laments, faded, it produced the aural illusion of moving further away. There was no Doppler effect at work here, but Siskin could not shake off the conviction that the voice emanated from a body in motion, one that had approached, passed overhead, and now travelled away from them. An aeroplane, then? Or something in orbit?

Tom was looking up at him, uncertainty and anxiety on his face. Siskin smiled, and as the voice faded back into the static hiss, he took his hand from the dial and placed it, carefully, tenderly, on the back of his sons neck. He felt the boy relax a little. Tom let out a sigh. Siskin breathed deeply and reached across to switch off the set.

"That's enough tonight, wouldn't you say?" he said. "Let's go in and have some cocoa. It's getting a bit late."

※

"These men stuffed with straw," said Mr Arkadin, smoke escaping in ropes from his nostrils. "Fools and parasites. Bedwetters who should never have left the nursery. They are not men. Thomas here has more sense of the world than they, is that not right, Thomas?"

Tom smiled and nodded.

"Of course. Prime Minister Thomas! It would be better. In Russia, there are men who lived through the fires of hell itself. Not the Georgian murderer Dzhugashvili, you understand. Not the foolish peasant who bangs his shoe upon the table in high company. No. Men of honour. Russians."

Arkadin paused to draw the last smoke from the cigarette, and ground it out.

"Heroes! Men like Gagarin. You know the first man to leave this earth was a Russian, Thomas? Of course you do. You read the magazines, and your father here, a man of learning, a man of science. Yes, I do feel proud of my countrymen when I hear the word cosmonaut..."

Tom turned in his seat at the table to look at his father, stationed as usual by the back door. Siskin nodded and reached to take the outhouse key from its hook.

"Don't forget to lock the door behind you," he said, and stood aside to allow Tom to pass.

While he extracted another cigarette from the package on the kitchen table, Arkadin looked up at Siskin and raised an eyebrow.

"Let Tom explain," said Siskin. The boy returned, and handed the keys to his father. He was carrying the Philips portable carefully under his left arm, hugged tight to the body.

"Well, this is a mystery, Thomas. You have my full attention."

Tom placed the Philips on the tabletop and press the rewind button. He expertly flicked between wind and playback to return to the correct point. Arkadin nodded in approval.

"Why don't you tell Mr Arkadin about it, Tom?" said Siskin.

"Well, you see, Mr Arkadin," said Tom quietly, "Dad and I were out in the outhouse listening to the radio. Oh, you know, not the BBC, not that kind of radio. The shortwave.

"We talk to people all over the world, don't we, Dad? It was a few days ago, Thursday I think? Thursday. We were in the outhouse and Dad warmed up the radio, and I was playing with this." Tom gestured to the Philips machine, and his face glowed red. Tom seemed to shrink into himself.

"What were you doing?" asked Arkadin.

"Oh, nothing. Just playing. Recording."

"I think he was being Dan Dare, Mr Arkadin," said Siskin. "A character. From the *Eagle*. Space pilot."

"Ah," said Arkadin, exhaling a cloud of smoke. "I see. Your comic books. The ones that you showed me before?"

Tom nodded, then with an effort, began again. "We started to hear a voice. It got louder and louder. We couldn't understand it, could we, Dad? It was a woman. It got louder and louder and then it went away, quieter and quieter."

"Very interesting," said Arkadin.

"Yes, and accidentally," said Tom, placing a finger precisely on the playback button, "we recorded what she said."

"And we thought that you might be able to tell us. Or perhaps what language she spoke," said Siskin.

"I am intrigued," said Arkadin. "By all means, let us hear it."

Tom clicked the playback button an adjusted the volume. From the machine's small speaker, a hiss emerged. "That's the sound of the radio," said Tom.

White noise began to form the rhythm of speech, the words that Siskin and Tom had played back a dozen times in the days since they had inadvertently recorded its passage.

Arkadin began to frown, and his hand fell slowly to the table, where the cigarette burned unregarded, as the woman's voice shouted in rage, before breaking up in static and emotion. It gained strength, yielded to panic and screams of torment or pain, then called again in hard clipped control, then finally turned to anger again as the voice began to fade to sharp ticks and crackles, then the flat white hiss.

Arkadin licked his lips, a deep rose colour against his grey beard and ashen skin. He deliberately, slowly, pressed the cigarette into the ashtray, then looked from Tom to Siskin. He jolted slightly as Tom switched off the tape machine.

"Do you know what she's saying, Mr Arkadin?" said Tom.

"Yes," said Arkadin, and coughed. "Yes, Thomas. The woman is Russian, my God."

"Can you tell us?" asked Tom.

Arkadin smiled slightly, then looked searchingly at Siskin.

No matter, thought Siskin. The boy should know. He nodded at the old man to continue.

"Please, Thomas, play it for me one more time," said Arkadin. "I will tell you what she says, translate for you, as we go along."

Tom found the started the recording and began playback. As the hiss rose from the speakers, Siskin could hear pop music coming from where Mary was watching "London Palladium" along the corridor, a pulse that, if he concentrated, slightly interfered with emerging voice from the Philips machine.

"Yes," said Arkadin. "I hear her counting, Five, four, three, two, one. Come in, she says, listen to me. She is hot. She breathes oxygen. 45, 50. She asks whether this is dangerous. The transmission begins now, she says. She grows angry. She condemns someone, a man called Korolev? You knew it was wrong, she says. Why won't they listen, she says. She is angry, yes, she curses some others, says they will see her in hell. 41. Oh, she is afraid. She can see flame. Again, the same. She is hot. She is hot. 32."

The voice began to fade into noise. Arkadin lent towards the speaker. As the signal dissolved, he sat back. Once more, he looked at Siskin a question in his eyes. Siskin nodded.

"It is difficult to say more," he said. "I find it difficult to have the words. I could hear the word crash, and something, a technical word. And then – there is no more." Arkadin picked up his cigarette packet, tapped the end on the tabletop, then carefully placed it flat on the surface. "This was on Thursday, you say?"

"Yes," said Siskin. "Very unusual. We don't usually pick up this kind of thing."

"No, I should hope not," said Arkadin. "Some voices are better left unheard, doctor. What was this... a ghost?"

Siskin shook his head, but Arkadin focused his attention on the boy.

"Russia is a land full of ghosts, young Thomas," he said. "It is becoming a little late, and I should go, but before I do, I will tell you a tale. A tale from my homeland."

Arkadin withdrew a cigarette from the case and lit it, inhaling deeply. "In a certain village in my homeland there was a girl called Mariia, known as Masha to her friends. This girl hated working, and would spend the days gossiping with anyone who would stand still. She decided to throw a party for her friends, where they would spin for her, and she would feed them. And in that way she would make up her share of the work.

"Late into the night, talk turned, as it does on cold winter nights, to ghosts and the dead. The girl Masha scoffed at her friends' fear and said that she wasn't afraid of anything.

"'Well, then,' said the spinners, 'go past the graveyard to the church, take down the holy picture from the door, and bring it back.'

"The foolish girl ran to the church, took down the picture, and brought it home. Her friends all recognised the holy picture and shook their heads. But the picture had to be returned, and it was past midnight."

Arkadin blew another cloud of smoke across the room.

"So, Masha went and put the picture back in its place. As she was passing the graveyard on the way back, she saw a seated corpse in a white shroud, gleaming in the moonlight. She went and snatched away its shroud. The corpse uttered not a word.

Back at home, the foolish girl said, 'There! I've taken back the picture and put it in its place; and here's a shroud I took away from a corpse.'"

Arkadin smiled gently and shook his head.

"And what do you think happened, Tom? After they had put away their spinning and lay down to sleep, the corpse tapped at the window and said: 'Give me back my shroud! Give me back my shroud!'"

Arkadin laughed, but there was an edge in his laughter that Siskin noticed, and he looked at his son. Tom was enthralled.

"Ha! The girls were so frightened they didn't know whether they were alive or dead. But the girl took the shroud, went to the window, opened it, and said: 'There, old ghost, take it.'

"'No,' replied the corpse, 'you must put it back where you took it from.' Just then the cocks began to crow. The corpse disappeared. The next night, the same thing happened. Masha offered the corpse its shroud, but it refused.

"After a few more nights of this, Masha's father and mother sent for the priest, told him the whole story, and asked him to help. Tell her to come to church tomorrow, he said.

"Next day the foolish girl went to church. Many people were there. The priest started the service, but as they were going to sing the Cherubikon, a terrible wind filled the church. All the people were knocked to ground, including the priest. All but one. That girl, that foolish girl, was caught up and down, above the heads of the people, whirled around and then flung to the ground. And she disappeared.

"There was one thing left. The handkerchief that had covered her hair. That handkerchief is still in that church, to my knowledge. Unless the Bolsheviks have removed it, of course."

✳

Some time later, Arkadin put on his bicycle clips, and Siskin and Tom accompanied him into the yard. They watched as the old Russian fixed a torch to the handlebars with a length of cord, and set the dynamo to the back wheel. As they did sometimes, they walked with Arkadin around the side of the house, down the front path, to where Siskin held the wicket gate open for bicycle and rider to pass through.

Tom and his father stood and watched as the old man pushed off, calling goodnight to all, and cycled slowly into the enveloping night, the red pulse of his rear light growing dimmer and dimmer until they could see it no longer.

"What happened to her, Dad?" asked Tom.

"I don't know, Tom," his father said. "I don't know."

Steadying himself on Tom's young shoulders, Siskin raised his eyes. He looked up at the infinite stars and their procession across the heavens; and beyond that was the pulse of the radio stars, the quasars, and beyond that, beyond the sound of the Earth's atmosphere and the travellers upon it, only silence.

Brian Baker teaches at Lancaster University, and has published critically on science fiction. He has recently published visual poetry works that interfere with HG Wells texts, such as Argo-0 (Steel Incisors) and An Invention (Trickhouse). This is his first fiction submission.

The 2025 Cymera Festival/ Shoreline of Infinity Short story competition for Scottish writers

Report by Noel Chidwick

The Winning Story is:
Dark Matter - Caitriana NicNeacail

Runners up:
Bibi's Sisters - Ailsa Fraser
The Story Collector - R.M. McRitchie

Highly Recommended
Gary's Massive Head Shouting Forever - Kieran McCaffrey
The fall of the anti-euthanasia collective - Mark Gallacher
Congratulations to all.

Here is the full longlist
Bibi's Sisters - Ailsa Fraser
Chronicles of the Train Delay - Ian Macartney
Dark Matter - Caitriana NicNeacail
Gary's Massive Head Shouting Forever - Kieran McCaffrey
Ideology - S.J. Ladds
Little Terror - Jon Reburn
Proceed Under Caution - Allan Tanner
Replaced - Kara Devlin
Sapience Record - Duncan Forgan
Sea Monkees - Sam Morris
The fall of the anti-euthanasia collective - Mark Gallacher
The Second Amen - Nicole Love
The Story Collector - R.M. McRitchie
The Weaver - Meghan Ellis

With grateful thanks to our judges, **Simon Spanton** and **Lorraine Wilson**, and **Ann Landmann** who maintained order.

Here are some of the comments from the judges as we battered our thoughts about.

S

"A great selection of stories. The common factor of downbeat world views was perhaps inevitable but the stories were all leavened by an awareness of the dramatic demands of the form, by fine description, some real wit and genuine empathy for fellow humans in extremis."

"What an amazing selection of stories! Thank you for a fabulous few days reading & agonising over these, it's been a struggle settling on the final 3"

"It was a REALLY good list. Stories and characters negotiating different ways of being human, of being alive and of dying."

"Genre fiction doing its job properly :)"

Here is what they said about the winning tales.

Dark Matter

This story is a perfect example of the way short fiction can contain universes. It spans, in poetic, delicately searing prose, both centuries and realities, altering our relationship with our world and its histories and leaving us deliciously side-eyeing the realm of quantum physics. A brilliant achievement.

The Story Collector

This had a lovely Ray Bradbury vibe (though with a possibly bleaker post-apocalyptic feel than Bradbury might have gone for). Really enjoyed the vivid descriptive writing, the focus on detail and the POV of the main character. It was the tattered but somehow magical feel of the world and the narrative that won me over. The fact that the story revolved around the importance of story even when everything else is gone was, for me, a powerful draw. Preaching to the converted given the audience for such a tale but no sledgehammer in the dealing.

Bibi's Sisters

A great bringing together of fairy tale's warnings about the patriarchy and Blade Runner's warnings about the dangers of flawed creators. Loved that it undermined the sentimental idea of the eccentric inventor tinkering in their garden shed so thoroughly. The dawning perspective of the POV character was neatly handled and their empathy with their sisters was tied touchingly to their inability to help. Pinnochio as seen through Black Mirror. A very effective story - controlled but with a real emotional punch nevertheless. And I loved the naming conventions of the sisters: the self-serving illusion of personality applied to a production line by the Maker.

Thanks to everyone who sent us a story.

Read Dark Matter →

Dark Matter

Caitriana NicNeacail

6th June 2025

Hedwig MacLeod balanced her cup of *renversé* on top of her open logbook, which was itself balanced on an uneven stack of papers on her desk. The milky fragrance of the coffee swirled and mingled with the smell of the office, the palimpsest of scent Hedwig had noticed in old physics corridors from Chapel Hill to China: a sharp musky funk, a tang of Van de Graaff generators and warm electronics and men's bathrooms and the pear-drop sting of acetone.

The screensaver bounced jaggedy-edged from one corner of the monitor to the other. Hedwig watched until it rainbowed from blue to purple before jiggling the mouse to wake the machine. Footsteps echoed from the corridor, and she turned to watch the walker pass the door, though she knew her officemates had all gone into town for cheap rotisserie chicken and Gamay de Genève. It was one of the janitorial staff. Not many of the postgrads or postdocs hung around CERN on a Friday night.

When the footsteps had passed, Hedwig turned back to the screen. She took a gulp of the coffee and re-read the email she'd written before dinner, her thumb hovering on the *Send* key.

To: thomson@phys.gla.ac.uk
Cc:
Attchmnt: <ford-lhcr3-dampe2023-params.txt>, <ford-output-1.txt>, <ford-output-1.png>
Subject: Ford Technique analysis of Run-3 v. DAMPE 2023

- - - - Message Text - - - - -
Hi Will,
I hope this finds you well. This email is probably going to sound a little crazy, so perhaps when you're back from Fermilab we can schedule a call and I can talk you through it in a bit more detail? I suspect there must be something off in my analysis, but I can't figure out what, or even if there was, how it could come up with output like this. But the alternative — that this is real — seems insane. I mean, there's no way that we'd just stumble on evidence for SUSY dark matter just like this, let alone that it would have these characteristics (?!??). It's got to be another raccoon-in-the-detector explanation. I just need a fresh pair of eyes on it, really.
You'll remember that at our last supervision meeting, you told me about the Ford analysis the IceCube guys did and suggested I have a go with LHC data. Well, I gave it a shot with the latest Run-3 dataset (using the St Denis reconstruction) cross-matched with last year's DAMPE

dataset. The parameters are in the attached file. And the output is in the other files.

You can see for yourself, but high-level summary: it looks for all the world like what a supersymmetric WIMP signal would hypothetically be like, but.. *signalling*. I mean, there's a kind of pattern, like, I dunno, if there were 2 people communicating in Morse code or something, if it were instantiated in dark matter. (I've taken to calling them Susy and Demi, haha ;-)

I know, that does sound crazy. I promise I'm not going off the deep end though. I know it'll turn out to be vibrations from roadworks or a micrometeorite shower hitting the DAMPE satellite or whatever. I just need to find out where the analysis has gone wrong, and this Ford method is so new none of the others can help, really. Hopefully it doesn't waste too much of your time!

Thanks so much,
Best regards,
Hedwig

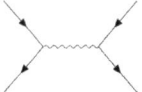

DEMI: *The threads glitter, spark and shimmer.*
SUSY: *The long-lived lattice shines with light.*
DEMI: *The one below the throne begs leave to weave a tale.*
SUSY: *Tell on.*
DEMI: *The one below the throne watches the world that wends the outer wheel. This one sees darkness, pain, evil, strife. Millions perish in photon blinks. Horror, void, screams, clawing, tearing, soul from skin, quark from squark. This one begs leave to cleave the*

evil, cleanse, remove, relieve, reweave. A target for our task, a cancer for our cask.

   SUSY: Granted. Let light shine brighter in the dark of night.

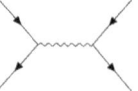

28th June 1914

A motorcade crawls crowded Sarajevo streets. An archduke waves, well-wishers cheer. A grenade flies. A fast-moving figure, faceless, flits like a phantom, kicks like a football player. The grenade falls in cold dark river water. The cars move on. The faceless figure slips unnoticed through the crowd. A young man sweats, hand slick on Browning pistol-grip. The phantom grabs him, drags him, dumps him deep in far-off forest. The archduke waves, well-wishers cheer.

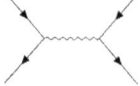

29th August 2016

"Hedwig!"

"Yes, miss?" Hedwig looked up from the sharp clean pages of the textbook, the smell of newness still rising from the paper. If she'd been on her own she'd have stuck her nose in the centrefold and sniffed it.

"What do you make of Holland's argument? That if the Archduke Franz Ferdinand had been more of a hawk than a dove, the Great War would have broken out much sooner than 1927 but potentially been less destructive?"

Hedwig looked at her book for inspiration, searching the grainy photo of the Archduke holding his Peace Prize medal outside the Nobel Institute in 1916. The Archduke's long-dead eyes looked back, black and white, but kept their counsel. She looked desperately at her friend Stella Campbell across the table, who was pointing her pen discreetly at the bullet-pointed box titled *The Great Man Theory*. Hedwig wished History had answers as clear-cut as Physics.

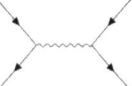

DEMI: *The threads glitter, spark and shimmer.*
SUSY: *The long-lived lattice shines with light.*
DEMI: *The one below the throne begs leave to weave a tale.*
SUSY: *Tell on.*

DEMI: *The one below the throne has worked the world that wends the outer wheel. This one has cleaved, reweaved, one war relieved. Yet threads rebound, the evil lives, renews, regrows, the ghosts yet scream, the war yet blooms in blood yet brighter than before. This one begs leave to deeper delve, matter mend, darkness dispel. A target for our task, a cancer for our cask.*

SUSY: *Granted. Let light shine brighter in the dark of night. But, child, take care. This weave is dark, the tangle tight. Some cancers deeper go, some worlds rewoven yet will broken be.*

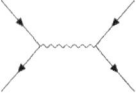

1st September 1784

A young man dismounts his horse, dusts the road from his coat. Pale stone shines in the sun, a hundred windows dazzle. A gate guard asks to see his papers. The young man proudly shows his entrance letter, his admission to the École Militaire. A boy leads him to the barracks. He breathes deep the scent of sweat, horse dung, gunpowder, power. He stretches full his short height, explores the halls where he will learn the secrets of strategy and fire. Two years to train, to learn to scale the heights, to show the world a Corsican can be king.

"M. Buonaparte?"

The young man turns. A messenger is holding out a letter, holding out a hand. The young man tosses him a coin, takes the wax-sealed envelope. His mother's hand. He reads, the words blur.

Napoléon, my son… your father… come home at once.

His hand shakes, his dreams crumble. No empire rises. Across the water, no naval push for innovation, no steam and iron revolution shakes the nations.

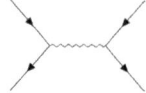

29th August 2016

"Hedwig!"

She froze, her finger marking her place on the thick yellow page. Late-afternoon sunshine slit the space between the curtains, dust motes spiralling like stars.

"Hedwig!"

Her mother's voice shrilled up the stairs, closer this time. Hedwig traced the curlicue of the calculus one last time before slowly shutting the book and replacing it on her brother's desk.

"Hedwig Marie-Eva MacLeod! These potatoes are not going to dig themselves out of the earth! And your father and brother will need their tea!"

"Coming, Mam!"

Hedwig stood, the coarse painted wood of the chair leg scraping on the floor. Her eye fell on the sheet of foolscap where James was drafting his university entrance essay.

Question 1: List and analyse the reasons why the Great Industrial Revolution started in Bohemia and Bavaria rather than in Western Europe.

A bitterness swelled in her stomach. In Bohemia, she'd read in the newspaper, girls could go to university too. Her brother would sail away next autumn, while she would milk the cows and care for Granny and the children until she was married off or died of consumption. She sighed and turned towards the stairs. Time to dig the potatoes, such as had survived the blight this year.

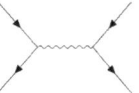

DEMI: The threads glitter, spark and shimmer.
SUSY: The long-lived lattice shines with light.
DEMI: The one below the throne begs leave to weave a tale.
SUSY: Tell on.
DEMI: The one below the throne has worked the world that wends the outer wheel. This one has cleaved, reweaved, some wars relieved, souls reprieved. Yet hunger and disease still bloom, spores spit, cells rot, choke, spot, dark tendrils curl, evils unfurl. This one begs leave to deeper delve, matter mend, darkness dispel. A target for our task, a cancer for our cask.

SUSY: Granted, but one last time. This weave is dark, the tangle tight. Some cancers call for stronger light than you or I can throw, some worlds rewoven yet will broken be.

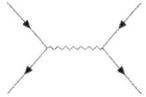

Summer, 2976 B.C.

A hunter crouches in a marsh, javelin poised. Mosquitoes buzz and whine. He scratches a welt. A movement in the reeds. The bronze-tipped weapon flies, pierces wet fur, warm veins, thin bones. The hunter strides the soggy clumps of grass, grabs the rodent corpse, stuffs it in his stash. The hunter homeward bound, a flea flees its dead host and hops towards the warmth of life. Bites. Its bacterial passengers bud, burgeon in the mathematics of mitosis. Mutate. Chromosomes copy, condense, cells split, one two four eight sixteen thirty-two sixty-four. The mutation propagates. The hunter shivers, warms in fever. Antibodies mobilise, immune cells gobble, phagocytise. Mutated, these bacteria are brighter, day-glo targets for the body's defences, rather than stealth fighters. The hunter wakes, feels fine, no sneeze or cough to spread Black Death, makes love, makes war, the population grows.

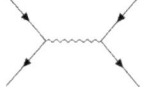

29th August 2016

"Hedwig!"

She glanced to her left. Sergeant Thomson beckoned, pointing down the trench. Regretfully, Hedwig stowed her data slate and turned on her HUD. Emission levels were nominal, radiation a little high, but no more than was expected this far into the Zone.

"Did you know that as early as the Bronze Age, they actually had a rather sophisticated system of mechanical calculation that eventually formed the basis of the first Industrial Leap?"

"Of course I know that," growled Sergeant Thomson. "I gave you that slate, remember? Much good it did them. Now shut up and keep moving. Can't let the Crawlers catch us out here."

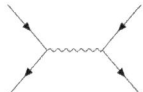

DEMI: *The threads glitter, spark and shimmer.*

SUSY: *The long-lived lattice shines with light.*

DEMI: *The one below the throne begs leave to weave a tale.*

SUSY: *Tell on.*

DEMI: *The one below the throne has worked the world that wends the outer wheel. This one has cleaved, reweaved, disease relieved. Yet...*

SUSY: *Yet?*

DEMI: *Yet failure follows. This one can but confess, the tangle is too deep, too dark for one to solve. My shame is offered up. The one below the throne will take the blame.*

SUSY: *Child, there is no shame in tackling a target for our task. This cancer ran too deep. Take heart, restart. Restore the lattice to its former state. This world we lift to stronger hands to save, this evil to more powerful to stave.*

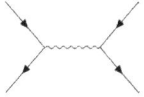

7th June 2025

Date: Sat, 7 Jun 2025 06:06:17 -0500
From: thomson@phys.gla.ac.uk
To: macleod@phys.gla.ac.uk
Cc:
Attchmnt:
Subject:: Re: Ford Technique analysis of Run-3 v. DAMPE 2023

- - - - Message Text - - - - -

Hi Hedwig,

Call me. Today, 12 noon GMT if possible. I'll be awake then. Heck, I'll probably be awake all night anyway, so just call me whenever you get this. I've run over your analysis and as far as I can see there aren't any glaring mistakes. This just ***might*** be our very first sign of supersymmetric dark matter. Of course it might turn out not to be, but we need to follow up ASAP. (And of course there can't be "entities" using it for communication, you've been reading too much sci-fi — but I've a tingling in my fingers that says this just might be the big break for SUSY DM.) I'm trying to get hold of Ford to run it by him as well. Anyway, CALL ME.

Cheers,
Will.

Caitriana NicNeacail is a Scottish speculative fiction writer from the Outer Hebrides. Her work is informed by her background in particle physics and in theology, along with the landscapes and languages of Scotland and China, where she spent many years. She loves Golden Age sci-fi and dreams of writing full-time some day.

A SHOWCASE OF SCIENCE FICTION, FANTASY AND SPECULATIVE FICTION BY SCOTTISH WRITERS

Iain Bain
John Buchan
Anne Charnock
Callum Dougan
Thomas Erskine
E.M. Faulds
Gwyneth Findlay
Lewis Grassic Gibbon
Pippa Goldschmidt
Rhiannon A Grist
T L Huchu
Chris Kelso
Ken MacLeod
Katie McIvor
R/L Monroe
Jeda Pearl
Rachel Plummer
Mark Toner
Kirsti Wishart

174 pages
Published in
paperback and digital
formats by

Who wrote the first Scottish science fiction book, published in 1817?

Available from
www.sfcaledonia.scot
10% discount code: shoscot

Hold The Chicken:
The Argument Against AI Art

Ruth EJ Booth

You can't have missed it. The Atlantic recently revealed that Meta is training AI on LibGen, a library of content scraped without permission from the internet, including the works of writers and academics across the globe.[1] Science Fiction authors are rightly up in arms.

You'd think that folks who describe the future for a living would be all for contributing to modern technology, but ironically, SF writers may be AI's most vehement critics. Why? Well, the answer is simple. It's bollocks. Allow me to clarify.

---

1 For the searchable list, see https://www.theatlantic.com/technology/archive/2025/03/search-libgen-data-set/682094/

Let's begin with the obvious issues around what we're labelling AI. Firstly, it's nothing of the kind, at least as we imagine it. Your own personal R2D2 is a way off yet. We're talking neural networks that use data to make predictions or content, depending on their design. Generative AI, like the Large Language Models on which ChatGPT and Grok are based, are fed large data sets and create text based on that. Want to write a novel, but can't find the time? Just tell ChatGPT your idea, and it'll do the rest.

Immediately, this throws up two issues for professional creators. Firstly, there's the whole rampant theft thing. Corporations have flouted international copyright law before, but rarely on this scale. Writers in the UK make barely £7,000 a year on average as it is.[2] And it's not as if this is a pdf torrented by some kid in Stockholm who can't use a library. It's wide-scale theft by a shmuck in Silicon Valley who doesn't value human labour. We see you, Zuckerberg. Noone buys that you were too broke to pay up.

And then there's the result. CEOs are falling over themselves to stuff the new hotness into anything they can, regardless of whether it's appropriate for the product or the market. Writers are losing side hustles in copywriting to AI that produces content without that pesky need for living expenses. But seemingly savvy early adopters are making a rod for their own back. Large Language Models depend on the data you feed them, lacking the discretion that human beings come with as standard. That's how we end up with legal trials citing fake cases, or recipes advocating wood glue on pizza. Small consolation for the creator victims of AI, but at the end of the day, you get what you pay for.

Neither of these endear the likes of ChatGPT to creatives, but is this enough to sour SF writers on a favourite trope? Boy, we love a bit of artificial intelligence, don't we? R2D2, Kryten, Hal 9000, the Terminator… Thinking machines have fascinated authors and enthralled audiences for decades. Even if today's AI isn't the real deal, it's a step in the right direction. Isn't it worth a little sacrifice to have your dreams come true?

Not if those dreams aren't what they seem. Cool stuff is cool, but when tech is the focus of a SFnal story, it's often less an attempt to predict the future, more an exploration of the present. Genre

2 According to the 2022 Creative Industries Policy and Evidence Centre study into Authors' Earnings in the UK.

authors like to extrapolate from current trends, moral standpoints, and so on to explore their consequences or implications. AI is rarely just AI. Martha Wells' *Murderbot* series is an exploration of neurodivergent experiences. *Red Dwarf* mechanoid Kryten features in storylines about exploitation, identity and more. Even Isaac Asimov's Four Laws were more thought experiments into the ethics of robotics than wish fulfilment. Fictional AI often tells us more about humanity than the machines themselves. Indeed, mainstream SF often depicts AI as a threat to humanity – see *Alien*'s Mother or *i ROBOT*'s VIKI. Not exactly a breeding ground for AI's biggest supporters.

So, AI doesn't have the best rep. We don't all have BB-8s – or even an edible meal – just yet. That doesn't make neural networks a write-off. Using limited data sets and statistical analyses, Predictive AI is already helping with vital scientific problems, from predicting natural disasters to the early detection of tumours. I doubt any SF authors believe AI won't save lives. But not all neural networks are put to such good use. It's difficult to argue that the price of artwork is as urgent a problem as curing cancer.

Creators of Generative AI might note the difficulties of making art – even professionals complain about that. Why not use AI and save yourself the labour? More art, more time for art. Generative AI makes skills available that otherwise take tens of thousands of hours to learn – time most people just don't have. And that's a fair complaint. It's why we have hired labour.

Experts train in their professions so you don't have to, then share that expertise for the price of living. When you pay creatives for art, you're not just paying for the result, but also the training you can't do. It's perfectly elegant. If saving money was the goal, you'd think tedious administrative tasks would be the first to be automated, rather than problems to which we already have solutions.

The content-generation argument for AI is based on a persistent and fundamental misconception about the difference between art as a skill and art as creative process. For example, most of us learn to write – that is, use tools to string together words and sentences – at school. To pay someone else to do that seems silly. If writing is something anyone can do, then the secret of storytelling must lie in great ideas. So why not have a machine write it for you? As long as

the ideas you give the machine are yours, then it's still your work.

Except that story ideas aren't the difficult part. Any author will tell you that they get hundreds per week. Give ten different writers the same idea and you'll get ten different stories – not just in style, but in theme, message, content. That's because all that time spent honing our craft wasn't just about technical skill. We were learning what makes a great story, how to confront narrative challenges, and most of all, how to use our experiences in crafting a truly unique voice on the page. There's a reason that copyright law is based on original work and design patents, not ideas. And AI simply cannot replicate originality.

Writers complain about writing largely because we're contrary sods who like a good rant. Often it's down to what's on the page not being as good as what's in our heads. Certainly, help with spelling and grammar might be welcome, but we don't want AI to do the work for us. When someone else writes the story, it ceases to be ours – legally, creatively, and fundamentally. Generative AI has nothing to offer artists except theft, poverty and creative destitution – and nothing to offer humanity but loss.

We haven't even touched on the environmental costs of AI, the huge amounts of electricity and water it requires, costs that mean this technology should surely only be used for the most vital of causes. Using AI to make art seems wildly counterproductive: a waste of resources that stunts the progress of humanity, based on greed and a fundamental misunderstanding of the creative arts. At a time when we don't yet have a cure for cancer, it's bizarre that corporations are so focussed on technology that could destroy livelihoods when instead they could be saving lives. You don't have to be Cassandra to see how bleak the implications are.

Quite apart from anything else, there's the indignity of knowing that the novel that you sweated and stressed over for years was stolen, scraped into a bucket with the rest of human endeavour, only to be dumped carelessly into the textual equivalent of a fried chicken processing machine. And it's not even good fried chicken. Human creativity is being sold for a poor imitation. It's cheap, it's bad for you, and ultimately the price will be way too high.

Ruth EJ Booth is a multiple award-winning writer and academic of fantasy based in Glasgow, Scotland. Her poetry and fiction can be found in *Black Static, Pseudopod* and *The Dark magazine*, as well as anthologies from NewCon Press and Fox Spirit Books. Winner of the BSFA Award for Best Short Fiction and shortlisted twice for the British Fantasy Award in the same category, in 2018 she received an honorable mention for Ellen Datlow's Best Horror of the Year, Volume 10. In 2019, her quarterly column for Shoreline of Infinity, 'Noise and Sparks', received the British Fantasy Award for Best Non-Fiction.

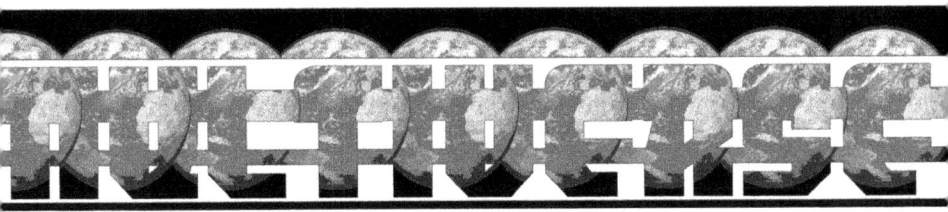

Like Shklovsky Making Strange

The future's poem occupied a spectrum
different to earthly light. Their tongue
followed a wilful and unlikely rhythm
as if their exobiological flesh
longed to pulsate, basking irradiated
beneath the trails of hurtling moons
on the edge of some cratered midnight
with lines breaking like the waves
of an ice-world's oceanic interior.

Their eyes glittered as beautiful as beetles
and their mutant opal-skin unfastened
like an obscure mechanism of the heart.
And this language we did not understand
rose in the air above us, levitating
like a luminous saucer.
While realists spoke of brick and soil,
the future danced to the colliding music
of singularities among the stars.

Oliver Smith

Oliver Smith is inspired by a joke of Tristan Tzara's, the future-pasts
of J G Ballard, and the landscapes of Max Ernst. His poetry has
appeared in many venues, including Abyss and Apex, Star*line, and
Strange Horizons. He holds a PhD in Literary and Critical Studies.
oliversimonsmith@outlook.com

Obsolete Horizons

I am only a mechanism of residual flesh
and some strange, lustrously-aged material
—a night-butterfly descended from the void.
All the others were left world-wandering dead,
their voices erased by expanding space.

I returned only as a ghost murmuring
in the garden's cypress-languor. From centuries
of icy quiet I raise my fingers,
micron by micron, torpid in the fading
gamma-ray flux of colliding galaxies.

My green skinned lover is less than dust,
a half-reptilian memory of debt accrued
on a distant world. Still, I remember friends
and comrades; the steadfast, the golden,
all the moss-grown graves. I left wasteland,

blasted and broken cities, planets extinct,
and suns extinguished, darkness triumphant.
At the end, I flew from the battlefields;
a ship lifted me free, quickening beyond
the tenuous membrane of atmosphere.

My coffin in the frost flew by the years
in gloom, travelling no faster than light.
I acclimatised to the sizzle and hiss
of evaporating stars in the rarefied night.
Now age has slowed me like dilated time.

Up past the ragged limestone scarp we wait
for some ancient signal; since I returned,
the stars grow scarce and are so far away.
The children look towards Andromeda and say,
"Curious, how we never heard of this war."

Oliver Smith

Captain Kirk visits my Daughter's Ballet Class

He's wearing more makeup than the teacher.
There's a tense moment when he walks in
and they stare each other down over skintight lycra
and enough bronzer to sculpt with.

My daughter is at least a head taller than any other girl in the class.
The other parents gather in small away teams,
leaving me in the corner in my bright red shirt.
The distance hurts. The pink satin skirts
twirl like nebulae; a galaxy
of tulle and lace, my daughter's face
locked on the teacher like a tractor-beam.

Kirk dances at the back of the class
and his feet stumble through every position.
He doesn't complain.
When it's time to pair up, none of the girls will go near him.
My daughter knows how it feels.
She shows him how to skide-skip, toes to heels,
in a diagonal line across the scuffed wooden floor
in time with the badly recorded piano music.

When they pass I hear him telling her
that childhood is an unpassable test,
and all that matters is how gracefully
you're defeated.

Afterwards I catch him
en pointe in the community centre carpark,
arms lifted in an arabesque.
The uniform is unforgiving.
My daughter holds his hand.

Rachel Plummer

Captain Kirk and the Intergalactic War against my Mental Health

He was always enterprising.
If there was a clean way out, he'd take it
but he wasn't above fighting dirty — sometimes the needs
of the many outweigh the few or the one and one
thing he taught me was how to let go
of the gravity holding me down.

He was there on the dark days, the gold
to my medical blues. The Kirkdays,
days that can't be replicated, when the stars fizz
like fists in a space station
bar brawl and Kirk
wants to split his lip on every single one.

Me and him, we go way back.
We've lost parts of ourselves to the black
between star systems that we'll never recover.
Survival shrinks us
to something that can slip between time and space
and still we come out fighting.

What I'm trying to say is
some things don't make it into the final report.
The admiralty can't understand
about hands and how they're dirtied
and how much red a shirt can hold before
the colour won't come out and stains what's in it.

Kirk's in this war to win it.
There's nothing lost that can't be found
on a planet far from home
and though he feels it like a punch
to the not insubstantial gut, what's coming up
on the starboard bow won't know what hit it.

He's always shot from the hip, paid lip
service to protocol, set phasers to listless.
He takes the universe in his arms
and kisses it, takes a shot
and never misses it

and if you could have one human in your corner
in a war they say is impossible to win
you could do worse than him.
Kirk knows the no-win.
Knows how to pry reality up by its edges
and redefine it.

If there's a way out, Kirk'll find it.
When the birds of prey are circling invisibly
and the galaxy isn't big enough
for us to share it peacefully
and Earth is just a dream that hangs impossibly
from empty space and can't be reached

he'll breach the peace,
he'll violate the neutral zone, send the thugs back home
no matter how tight they cling on to existence.
Kirk takes my hand in his. In the distance
stars die, and from their ash new worlds will form.

Rachel Plummer

Rachel Plummer is a recipient of the Scottish Book Trust's New
Writers Award for poetry, and has had work published in a range
of journals and anthologies. Their first book, Wain, is a collection of
LGBTQ+ retellings of Scottish folklore. Their latest poetry collection,
Once I Carried Three Crows, is published by Tapsalteerie. Rachel
lives in Edinburgh with their two children, three guinea pigs, and
entirely too many books.

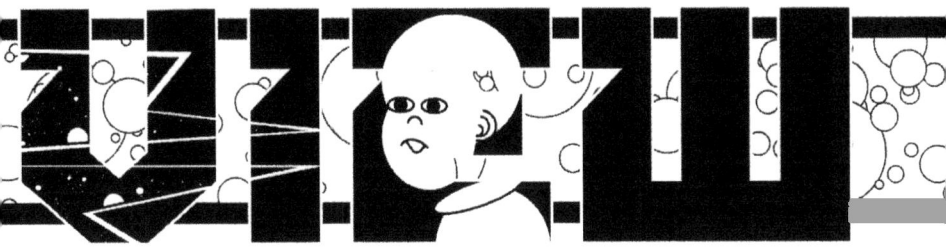

Eugen Bacon

Converses with Pippa Goldschmidt

This issue of Shoreline features an article by the hugely distinguished and multi-talented author Eugen Bacon, and I was thrilled to be able to catch up with her and ask her a few questions about her work.

Pippa Goldschmidt: Your CV is incredibly impressive, you have qualifications in computer science as well as a PhD in creative writing. Does your scientific/academic expertise feed into your writing? If so, how?

Eugen Bacon: I get that question a lot. Recently, as part of a seminar series on Applied African Speculative Fiction, how we can use storytelling in research, policy and activism, I shared how I increasingly

imagine the impacts of technology in transforming environments and people on the continent and beyond. You can watch the video Art and Science: The Marriage of Figaro online.

I was once a scientist and now I am an artist. In a mode of auto-ethnography, I learn from the self as data. I love playfulness with text and curiosity with art of telling stories differently. For example, 'Industrial Pleasure', published

Danged Black Thing Eugen Bacon

in my short story collection *Chasing Whispers* by Raw Dog Screaming Press, is a fun story with a theme of futures energy. African migrant Mayasa is sick of scrubbing pots and cleaning out toilets for cheap labour, and discovers—through an ad 'Hankering for money? That's all in the past.'—how she can safely sell her pleasure to a company that has unravelled a revolutionary source of renewable energy, using a woman's climax on a collecting drum.

In 'Unlimited Data', published in my collection *Danged Black Thing*, I again borrow from my computing background to write the story of an illiterate woman in the village whose husband coerces her into being a test subject for a program that comes in the form of a Bluetooth chip inserted into a woman's body, connecting with his smart phone, and he never needs to buy data bundles again—it all comes with the chip. Naturally, there are irreversible consequences on the wife.

Science has taught me structure, persistence in research, organised scepticism, curiosity, attention to detail, adaptive persistence and a 'solutions' focus. Art has taught me passion, aesthetics, vision, creativity, inherent meaning, diversity, uniqueness and the non-linear. The scientist learns from the artist who is a mother, a woman, a writer, an editor, a scholar, a colleague, a mentor, a friend.

Pippa: You were born in Tanzania and you lived in the UK before moving to Australia, and I think you speak more than one language. So, perhaps similarly to the first question about your academic roots, your geographic roots are widespread - how do they influence your writing?

Eugen: I speak and think in Swahili and English, understand several African dialects, mostly Bantu, and can ask for a glass of water in French. My hybridity as an African Australian was once a struggle as I sought to find a sense of belonging. My lived experience is of a person betwixt and between worlds, a self-made refugee in what ethnographer Dwight Conquergood in his article 'Rethinking Ethnography: Towards a Critical Cultural Politics' calls a 'postmodern existence of border-crossing and life on the margins'.

This has greatly influenced my writing where, first, it was a self-interrogation, a quest to understand, to belong, to come to terms with myself, with others, and with the world around me.

For a long time, overseas, I struggled with my identity—I was trying to be African, trying to be Australian. No one said to me, 'Why can't you be both?' And then I started writing Black people stories, because I wanted to 'write myself in', like Octavia Butler. I wanted to write stories where characters looked like me—brown-eyed, tight curly haired—not blue-eyed, blonde. The act of heroing Black protagonists was like coming out, a discovery of the self.

My writing is still a curiosity—a product, a process, a form of invention and an instrument of reflection, as another writer, Julia Colyar examines in her article 'Becoming Writing, Becoming Writers'. My writing is a method of inquiry as a means of illustration.

'I write to answer incipient questions that trouble my mind … I write to relieve some form of anxiety, the question of anxiety being the unanswerable question … since the object cause of anxiety… cannot be symbolized … In this sense, I write because I must do so, exhilarating, detestable or painful though this might be.'

These are the words of Dominique Hecq, a scholar,

friend, mentor who looked at the potential usefulness of psychoanalysis for the creative writer. Her words speak personally to me.

I write cautionary tales or narrative of hope, where I hero Black people stories. I am a person from a culturally diverse background and—on the giving and receiving end, as a writer who is also an editor—it's important for me to be aware of the risk of silencing or removing an author's cultural or other distinctiveness.

It's crucial that we embrace unique voices and encourage difficult conversations, including pointing out bigotry or hate when we see it. A passive onlooker is an agreeable participant.

Pippa: And finally, do you have any new work appearing in the near future?

Eugen: I have two books out this September, *Novic* by Meerkat Press and *The Ngaꞌphandileh Whisperer*, an Afrocentric story set in the Sauútiverse. Stoked about both!

119

Editor's intro: Eugen Bacon is hugely experienced at both writing and editing. Here she shares some of her experiences in writing to commission.

So You Have Been Commissioned to Write a Story...

Eugen Bacon

As you become increasingly published and catch the eye of publishers and editors, you start receiving invitations to write commissioned stories for anthologies, or perhaps as a feature story for a publication.

The best type of commissioned story is an invitation to send in a reprint for consideration – a story already exists. You just have to choose the right story from your published works. This might happen for a 'year's best' anthology that an editor is soliciting stories for.

Original stories are another beast. You are writing to someone else's muse, penchant and timeline. They have conjured themes that may range from unlimited futures, hard science fiction with a focus on planets, soil, oceans, space opera noir, climate change ten years from now... all examples of some themes I've encountered, and the list is endless.

Writing a commissioned story to a specific theme can be particularly difficult if you're an immersive writer like me, where you must feel the story, be the story, and connect with its characters for it to succeed.

You write at your best and invent your best stories, when you believe in your characters, their motives, their relationships and the events you're creating. The secret, I discovered, is to leave the story a bit as you contemplate the theme, let the idea simmer in your head until someone else's muse becomes your muse.

Both spending some time with the story in your head, and doing the hard work in researching the theme is invaluable in helping you write to the editor's specification. There's the editor's deadline that doesn't care whether you're a pantser or plotter, are in the glums about pandemic lockdowns, or you have a novel to finish. It also takes knowing yourself, understanding the kind of things you're excited writing about, and knowing when to say to an editor, *No, maybe next time.*

I have had two flops – three if I am to count a commissioned essay. The first commission was to a broadly-themed speculative anthology I should have aced at submitting to, but my mind was fatigued. I'd just released a novella and two collections of short stories, and was in the middle of writing stories for a new collection. I needed to determine if I wanted to release my original stories aimed for the collection into the anthology, knowing I could no longer use them in my collection if they were accepted, because (1) the contractual exclusivity period for the anthology was long and (2) the publication date was far.

I decided to write a new story but it struck me after I'd clicked *submit* (right?!) that my piece was literary and beautiful, just not speculative enough. The editors were open to giving another submission a go, and the second story I wrote just didn't work for their vision, however broad. I cut my losses, and successfully integrated the work as an original story in my collection *Chasing Whispers* by Raw Dog Screaming Press.

The second commission was rather attractive as it was for a major publisher. It was a sequel to an anthology I had written about in my scholarly essays on black speculative fiction and Afrofuturism. I wrote what I felt was the perfect science fiction story about AI and belonging, and it aligned with the theme. But the story was also superb for my collection, and I believed I had ample time to write a new one. I did, but I'd already committed the unforgivable sin of withdrawing a story (aka burning bridges with publishers and editors), which put me on the wrong foot with the editor.

When I sent in my new offering, a fantasy story about gods and war, the editor was not open to it, and the criticism was personal and brutal. I offered to write a revision, based on their feedback, but it was no surprise when a rejection arrived many months later, by which time I had already figured out the inevitable, and expanded the story into a new novella, *Broken Paradise*, that was shortlisted in the BSFA Awards, Shirley Jackson Awards and Nommo Awards for Speculative Fiction by Africans.

The third commission was not to write a story but an essay for an 'elite' Australian magazine. The editor wanted me 'to explore the ideas around space and colonisation, especially work (literature, pop culture, etc) that counters colonial tropes and offers new possibilities'. They wanted something on Afrofuturism and space colonisation. I was too eager to ask enough questions or the right questions. I wrote along lines that I thought addressed the editor's specificity.

They didn't.

It just didn't work with this editor, and I suspect some differences were cultural: trying to put me in a box as a spokesperson for black people, where the blackness was unclear. Australia has Indigenous Peoples – and that is the type of blackness that people seem to understand, not the cultural or migrant story from Africa or the diaspora. The editor wanted me to include perspectives of First Nations People, which simply was not my story to write.

But I've had successes, numerous commissioned stories still being released in anthologies. The most fun I had was on a story for a fantasy anthology from the perspective of an animal protagonist. Other contributors had written on the perspective of the horse of the Headless Horseman, a fey hound of the Wild Hunt, a werewolf shunned by his tribe for changing... I scratched my head on this one, nearly declined the invitation, then the idea of a story in an African village where a raven wants to become a witchdoctor's familiar struck in a metafictional way:

"Once upon a world lives a raven that loves to watch. It's at a time of the pandemic[1], so the watching can only be in social or physical distance[2], and in human person-lengths.

Ja is perched on a low-hanging branch, and not standing on a sill, because this is a village, not a town or a city. She's looking at a river of villagers trickling in and out of an old witchdoctor's hut in a slow-moving queue.

The witchdoctor's name is Knuckles. He has one blue eye and a black one. He has many totems to commune with the dead..."

I have since then written two other stories featuring the same witchdoctor Knuckles, his apprentice Sita, and Ja, the raven, one recently in a Norse mythology anthology, where a death maiden on sabbatical finds herself in the village.

Another commission I had a blast with was for a Sherlock Holmes

---

1 The world is in the throes of grappling with Covid-19, and only itinerant folks nomadic across Woop Woop or Turkmenistan may be oblivious of the virus.
2 Whatever you want to call it—anything that makes you feel good about a bad situation, you-know-what-I'm-saying?

anthology, where—the guidelines determined—Sherlock had to be a woman, and there had to be a Watson. In this multiverse story set in the Afrocentric Sauútiverse, sleuth Shaalok Ho-ohmsi and her ward Wa'watison are summoned to the planet Ekwukwe to solve a mystery of vanishing echoes. I liked it too much and withdrew it from the commissioned anthology, and published it as an original titular story 'The Mystery of a Place Between Waking and Forgetting' in my collection *A Place Between Waking and Forgetting*, both longlisted in the BSFA Awards.

To atone for my greed, I wrote a new story for the commissioned anthology, *Sherlock is a Girl's Name*, this one casting our Black protagonist in an African setting. In this story, the once great sleuth Shalok Homsi is suffering from the worst possible case of pandemic blues and is not at her best. She travels to Pemba Island in East Africa with her orphaned ward Watison, keen to recuperate from a gnarled mental state, unaware that a mystery is waiting for her to solve at her chosen beach lodge. The story is a first-person 'you' narrative, where the narrator Shalok is addressing an invisible reader, and Watison:

> "I am Shalok Homsi—I don't keep a circle. Just you, dear Watison."

As you can see, another editor's muse can be a blessing in the types of stories it whispers to you. The plus side of being commissioned to write is that the approach is already a positive thing: the publisher or editor is interested.

It's like a hiring manager inviting you to submit a job application for an open role. If they don't like the first pitch, they might ask for another one over a cuppa.

Own it. Make it your story. Write to word count, theme and deadline.

Believe in the story, and believe in you, because the publisher or editor already does or wants to. The odds are in your favour—don't stuff it up.

Eugen Bacon is an African Australian author. She's a Solstice, British Fantasy and Foreword Indies Award winner, a twice World Fantasy Award finalist, and a finalist in the Shirley Jackson, Philip K. Dick Award, and the Nommo Awards for speculative fiction by Africans. Eugen is an Otherwise Fellow, and was also announced in the honor list for 'doing exciting work in gender and speculative fiction'. Visit her at eugenbacon.com.

REVIEWS

I Nova Scotia Vol. 2,
I New Speculative
I Fiction from Scotland
I **Editors: Neil Williamson and Andrew J. Wilson**
I Published by Luna Press, 2024
I £16.99 paperback
I **Review by Duncan Lunan**

Nova Scotia Vol. 2 continues the tradition of producing a new volume of speculative fiction by Scottish writers each time the World Science Fiction Convention comes to Glasgow, its predecessors being *Shipbuilding* (1995) and *Nova Scotia* (2005). As the editors say, "The contributors are all Scots. They're Scottish in the broadest sense: some were native-born while others have chosen to make their home here; some are highlanders, others urbanites; and this gives us an extraordinary range of perspectives."

There are 26 contributors in all, which makes it impossible to give due credit to each story within the confines of a normal review. Looking for recurring themes, there's retribution for past injustices, particularly to women, as in "Mhairi Aird" by Lorraine Wilson, and in "Broderie Ecossaise" by Eris Young. There are new technologies which change everything, as in Ken MacLeod's "Weak Gods of Mars" and David Goodman's "New Town", and new takes on ideas which have been around for a long time, like Russell Jones' "Blood Lines" and Lindz MacLeod's "Junior". Several of the stories, like Jon Courtenay Grimwood's "Me, and Not Me", feature police investigations into what appear to be crimes, including murders, but turn out to be something different, at least in means and motivations. That one and Andrew J, Wilson's

"The Bruce and the Spider" are set in alternative histories, Scotlands that never were, because Robert the Bruce was helped by extraterrestrials and because Bonnie Prince Charlie won; whereas Pippa Goldschmidt's "Lise and Otto" probes Otto Hahn's feelings as science in Germany comes under Nazi control, in the build-up to World War 2 and beyond. Dilys Rose's "The Colour of Their Eyes" is also about the breakdown of a relationship between researchers, this time on a remote Scottish island rather than in a totalitarian state. On a different note, Ali Maloney's "Grimaldo the Weeping" is set in a world where magic works, more's the pity, and recalls the 'Dying Earth' stories of Jack Vance. The Earth is dying in a different way during Rhiannon A. Grist's "Dodos", where attempts to resurrect dodos and save whales are taking place against a Voluntary Human Extinction Programme - and not everyone is happy with that. "Under the Hagstone" by Doug Johnstone has Edinburgh similarly ruined by the arrival of an extraterrestrial artefact, and the last story, "To the Forest" by Jeda Pearl, features 'floral emancipation' and 'plantlife personhood'.

These brief allusions to the stories don't begin to deal with them at the level they deserve, and some, like Grant Morrison's "Peter's Thoughts" and C.L Hellisen's "Sugar

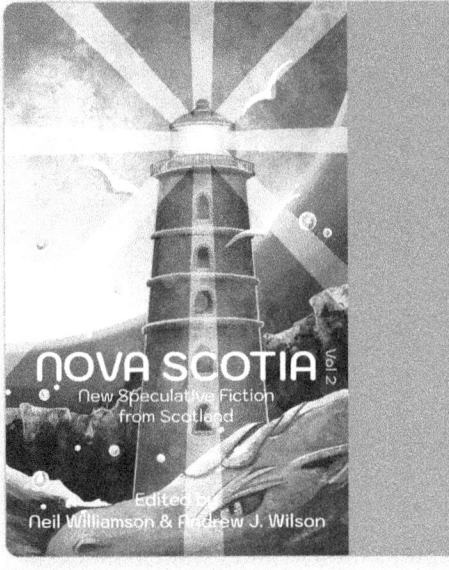

Teeth" don't lend themselves to that treatment at all, and nor does Neil Williamson's "Midnight Flit", despite its brevity. Even shorter is Ever Dundas' "Helpline Zero", a heavily redacted one-page government document about a new pandemic, which does for such communications what Richard Hammersley did years ago for similar ones about warfare. Among several stories about the trials faced by immigrants to Scotland, at various periods, "Love, Scotland" by E.M. Faulds shows them and other minorities being pushed into enclaves as the Scots fall progressively for the rhetoric of a right-wing English government.

But the book's scariest story comes shortly before the end, and I should explain that 50-odd years ago I had a supernatural experience in Glencoe which remains with me as if it was yesterday. In "Glencoe" by E.M. Faulds, an abusive father and his victimised daughter come off the road there, by night, and have to seek shelter. The father gets his comeuppance, but the daughter isn't safe either. Some details of this story are so familiar that I wonder if E.M. Faulds, like me, has had to go through the Coe, by night, at low revs and in freezing fog, but pressing on because stopping seemed like a very bad idea. In those conditions, physical and mental, don't go there.

The first ever anthology of SF by Scots was *Starfield, Science Fiction by Scottish Writers*, which I edited for Orkney Press in 1989 and re-edited for Shoreline of Infinity in 2018. While doing so I found online a review which was published by the British Science Fiction Association at the time, titled "Why Did They Bother?", arguing that if one was to have an anthology of SF by Scots, one by hairdressers might as well come next. By contrast, when I showed the second edition to a friend with a better knowledge of Scottish literature, his comment was, 'My God! Alasdair Gray, Edwin Morgan, Naomi Mitchison, Janice Galloway... how did you pull this off?' (to which my answer was that I knew most of them beforehand).

It has to be said that the first edition sold poorly, largely due a perception then - in Scotland as well as beyond - that 'if it's Scottish, it has to be parochial'. In the Preface to the second edition, I wrote, 'Very definitely, that's no longer the case'. But the Introduction to *Nova Scotia Vol 2* is headed 'Wha's Like Us?', and if there are any remaining pockets of prejudice against SF by Scots, it's clear that the editors and the contributors do not care the proverbial docken.

Starfield, Science Fiction by Scottish Writers, edited by Duncan Lunan and including the story 'Big Fives' by Richard Hammersley, was reprinted by Shoreline of Infinity and is available now. Details of it and Duncan's other books are on his website,

www.duncanlunan.com

The Utopia of Us
Editor: Teika Marija Smith
Published by NewCon Press in August 2023

Review by AJ Deane

The Utopia of Us is a 2024 anthology inspired by, and a tribute to, Yevgeny Zamyatin's novel *We*. Published in 1924 and written shortly after the devastation of World War I, which left much of Europe and Russia reeling, *We* was a groundbreaking book; it is widely considered one of the grandparents of the dystopia genre, influencing George Orwell's *1984* and *Animal Farm*, Ray Bradbury's *Fahrenheit 451*, and many others, and has been a touchstone for writers ever since.

The Utopia of Us features stories by some big names, including Adrian Tchaikovsky, so I was hopeful it would be good – I was not disappointed. As always with an anthology, I found some of the pieces stronger than others, but they were all of a very high standard and there is much to enjoy, if 'enjoy' is the right word for reading some disturbingly all-too-believable glimpses of potential futures. Brutal, surprising, full of despair and hope, awe and wonder, it is a well-compiled rollercoaster ride. Any book where you have to pause to digest what you've just read is doing well, and there is much of that here. There are, by its tributary nature, some references and characters who featured in *We*, but you don't need to have read that first – though I suspect you might want to afterwards. I shall highlight a few of my favourites, though I enjoyed them all, and the range is so good there is something for everybody.

The collection starts strong with the excellent *Intrinsic-Extrinsic-Terrific* by Aliya Whiteley, which owes much of its Totalitarian State interference and intrusion

THE UTOPIA OF US

An anthology inspired by Yevgeny Zamyatin's *We*
Edited by Teika Marija Smits

ANNE CHARNOCK • RAYN EPREMIAN • R. T. ESTER
LIAM HOGAN • TIM MAJOR • NADYA MERCIK
FIONA MOSSMAN • ANNA ORRIDGE • SOFIA SAMATAR
ANA SUN • ADRIAN TCHAIKOVSKY • MICHAEL TEASDALE
DOUGLAS THOMPSON • IAN WHATES • ALIYA WHITELEY

into everyone's everyday lives to both *We* and *1984*. Any readers familiar with riding an underground rail system would be forgiven for immediately identifying with the feel of the story, and the similarities to some places around the world today, or the direction in which some countries are going, should be very apparent.

My next two selections leant more into the hopeful side of things; *The Earth Heals-Silent Days-Vagaries and Savagery* by Anne Charnock, has more than a little of the bittersweet eco-SF feel of the film *Silent Running*, though it is by no means unoriginal or less impactful for that. *A Peculiar Job-The Wash-Somebody Waiting for Me* is a cyberpunk-esque offering from Liam Hogan, which looks at alienation, human connection, and love in an increasingly online-yet-disconnected world. A timely tale if ever there was one.

As a Dungeons & Dragons fan, I found myself caught by the random choice hook of the protagonist in Ana Sun's *Anatomy of Emotion-The Carving of Chance-Seize the Moon* (the iconic icosahedron twenty-sided die, or D20).

The book finishes with a story which could probably do with a re-read after digesting *We*, if you haven't read it before enjoying this. Sofia Samatar's *The Integral-True Literature-Everything is Blooming* makes some strong references to Zamyatin's novel in a clever archaeological and historical documentary of the original work.

The Utopia of Us is an enjoyable read with a wide take on how the authors have chosen to respond to Zamyatin's *We*, and I think he would have enjoyed all the stories contained in it – despite perhaps being horrified that the philosophical, ethical, environmental and governmental warnings are still necessary, one hundred years later.

More reviews online
we publish new reviews regularly on our website.

Shoreline of Infinity is based in Edinburgh, Scotland. Shoreline of Infinity Science Fiction Magazine is a print and digital magazine published in PDF, ePub and Kindle formats. It features new short stories, poetry, art, reviews and articles.

But there's more – we run live science fiction events called Event Horizon, with a whole mix of science fiction related entertainments such as story and poetry readings, author talks, music, drama, short films – we've even had sword fighting.

We also publish a range of science fiction books; take a look at our collection at the Shoreline Shop. You can also pick up back copies of all of our issues. Details on our website...

www.shorelineofinfinity.com

The SF CALEDONIA

SF Caledonia is a space for Scotland to show off its talented community of science fiction/ speculative fiction/ fantasy writers to the world – and beyond. It's a website designed to be easy to read on any device, no app necessary. It's free to read, and you don't need to subscribe. There are videos of readings of some of the stories.

New serial: *The Pocketbook Guide to Scottish Superheroes by Kirsti Wishart*

When we invited Kirsti to send us a story for SF Caledonia she also asked if we were interested in a novel she had written, but not yet published. *It's about an alternative Scotland where folk randomly develop superpowers,* she said. We're not really *geared up for publishing full length works, we* said, *but if you're willing to experiment, how about releasing it as an online serial on SF Caledonia?*

To our delight, Kirsti said *yes,* and reworked it into a serialised format. We began publishing in May 2025. We publish episodes twice a month, and you can catch up at any time.

Go to www.sfcaledonia.scot and join us at

Chapter 1 –
A rude awakening? – Swarming superheroes – a blast from the past

---

.**Nominate a Scottish writer.**

You can nominate a Scottish writer of science fiction, fantasy or speculative fiction to SF Caledonia. They can be past or present – we are aiming to include *all* published Scottish SF writers.

Go to the website and you'll find a link to a nomination form, asking for a few details about the writer and yourself, in case of any follow-up questions.

www.sfcaledonia.scot

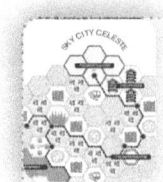

The Botanist of Sky City Celeste

Lyndsey Croal

Stepping off the elevator platform, I can't help but stop to take in the view of the city. Around us, artificial trees stretch up so far, their canopies almost reach to the top of the glass dome. Each outward branch of the structure hosts an array of greenery making the forest illusion more convincing...

sfcaledonia.scot/urls/sky

Captain Kirk visits Edinburgh in August

Rachel Plummer

He beams himself up
town to where it's busiest.
The people of this planet like to congregate
in places of religious significance
such as bus stops...

sfcaledonia.scot/urls/kirked

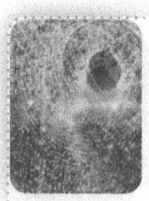

t/r/oll

Chris Kelso

Just want to report a possible intruder moving across front lawn at Mapplethorpe Lane, Arlington. Ten notifications have popped up on my smartphone saying...

sfcaledonia.scot/urls/troll

www.sfcaledonia.scot